MY ALMOST EX

PIPER RAYNE

Cover Photo: Regina Wamba

Cover Design: By Hang Le

1st Line Editor: Joy Editing

2nd Line Editor: My Brother's Editor

Proofreader: My Brother's Editor

About My Almost Ex

In the middle of a crowded bar in our small Alaskan town, my estranged wife snuggles up to me as if we're still a happy couple.

Don't get me wrong, we were a happy couple—before she walked out on me a year ago. We were the high school sweethearts everyone thought were destined to be together forever. We thought so too, which is why we married shortly after graduation.

We had a good marriage. Until she left me without any real explanation.

Now, she's back—and this is the real kicker—she has amnesia and thinks I'm still her husband. Technically I am, although the divorce papers are sitting at the lawyer's office.

She's desperate to remember her life in Sunrise Bay but I only want to find out why she left me. Once we conjure that memory up, it's sayonara because there's no second chances here. But as you probably already figured out, things didn't go quite as I planned.

my almost EX

<u>**The Greenes**</u>

<u>**Hank's Kids**</u>
Cade Greene (31)
Co-owner Truth or Dare Brewery
Fisher Greene (29)
Sheriff
Xavier Greene (27)
Pro Football Player
Adam Greene (25)
Forest Ranger
Chevelle Greene (24)
Water Boat Tourist

<u>**Marla's Kids**</u>
Jed Greene (31)
Co-owner of Truth or Dare Brewery
Nikki Greene (28)
Radio Host
Mandi Greene (26)
Owner of SunBay Inn
Posey Greene (22)
Owner of Fringe

<u>**Hank and Marla's Kid**</u>
Rylan Greene (11)

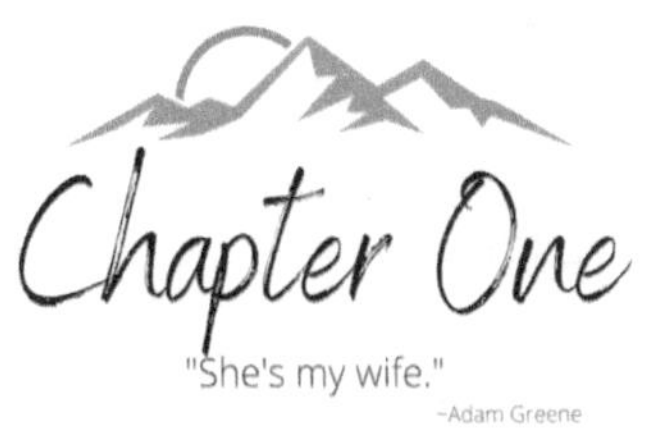

Adam

"**D**id that woman just call you babe?" my new girlfriend, Alicia, asks with a 'what the hell' tone.

My mouth is too dry to answer her question. I can't stop staring at "that woman," aka Lucy, and my thoughts are racing faster than an Indy car.

Before you assume I'm an asshole who cheats on his girlfriend, know I'm not. A year ago, the woman who just called me babe—my wife—walked out on me without any explanation. Now, after I've pulled myself from the depths of depression and tried to move on with my life, she approaches me at my brothers' brewery as though we're still married. I haven't seen or spoken to her since she left.

If you want to be technical, she *is* still my wife. She never sent divorce papers, and it wasn't until last week that I went to the town lawyer and asked him to start the process of drawing up papers.

Alicia clutches my arm because I still haven't taken my

eyes off of Lucy. My estranged wife is flitting around my family, hugging everyone and conveying how much she's missed them, pausing at my brother Cade's new fiancée, Presley. We're supposed to be celebrating their engagement right now. Good thing Cade's used to plans never going the way we expect—as often happens with a family as big as ours.

I spot Lucy's mother, Susan, push through the crowd of gawkers in the brewery. Everyone's whispering and staring at us. There couldn't be a worse time for Lucy to show up out of the fucking blue.

"Susan?" I say because I'm hoping she has an answer as to why Lucy's acting as if we're still happily married. She doesn't answer immediately, her concerned gaze focused solely on her daughter. The look is alarming enough to suggest there's a missing puzzle piece that makes my stomach clench. "What the hell is going on?"

Susan's gaze flickers to mine. She scolds me with her narrowed eyes, but her shoulders fall. "She suffered an accident and... she lost her memory, Adam. She has amnesia."

"So?" I ask.

Alicia's breast brushes along my bicep as though she's afraid I'm going to get away.

"She thinks you're still happily married."

My stomach clenching turns to full-on nausea. Married we are, but definitely not happily.

"You're married?" Alicia asks, her arm winding out of mine.

I run a hand through my hair, looking to my father to somehow fix this for me. "Technically, yes."

"And you failed to ever mention this to me?"

The last person I have time for conflict with right now is

Alicia. We've barely begun dating. Seeing her has been my first attempt to put myself out there since Lucy left.

"Excuse me." Lucy comes back over and nudges between Alicia and me. She always was good at making sure people knew I was hers. If I wanted to go down memory lane, I'd remember that it was something I loved. "Who's this girl?" she whispers in my ear.

"Lucy, we should go." Susan takes Lucy's hand and attempts to pull her along.

"Why would I leave? Look, I found Adam." Just as Lucy's gesturing toward me, her smile dims and she looks at her mom. "Wait... you mean..."

"You and Adam are no longer together," Susan says.

A strangled cry leaves Lucy and she removes herself from me. "Oh."

Lucy looks at Alicia as though she's the reason we're not together, causing fury to build in my chest. She should look in the mirror if she's wants to see who is to blame.

My entire family stands there speechless, a small miracle in itself. I guess it takes a woman with amnesia to silence them. Maybe not the best time for a joke, but I have no idea how to handle this situation. The despair in Lucy's eyes is killing me. A huge part of me wants to fix it for her, tell her she can have me if she wants. But what would that solve? The damage was done a year ago and there's no coming back from it.

She points at Alicia. "Are you Adam's?"

"We need to go. I'm so sorry." Susan urges Lucy to her side. "Have a good night."

I open my mouth to say something, though I don't know what, then shut it, watching them leave. Alicia cuddles up to my side again as though we're going to carry on with our night as planned. It all feels wrong now.

"I'll be back," I say, dislodging myself from Alicia.

"I thought he was just going to stand there." Cade says it as though that would be the worst thing in the world.

I owe Lucy nothing. She's the one who broke *my* heart. So she had an accident and lost her memory. That's not my business, nor my problem anymore. At least I tell myself that as I wind through the crowd, catching up to Susan and Lucy on the cobblestone road outside the brewery. Susan has her arm around Lucy's shoulders and they're whispering as more people try to stop them to say hello.

"Lucy!" I yell.

All the hustle and bustle of the celebratory night before tourist season kicks off halts, leaving a deafening silence blanketing the square.

Lucy slowly turns. I slow my steps and narrow the distance.

Before I reach her, Susan steps between us, putting her hand out to stop me. "Please don't, Adam. This doesn't change what happened between the two of you. I'm sorry for interrupting your night, but this isn't a good idea."

Lucy wipes tears from her eyes with the back of her hand, and my jaw clenches at seeing her upset even if I wish it didn't. I lean to the side to get around Susan, but she steps in front of me again.

"She's my wife," I say.

Susan gives me a look to say we both know she's not.

"You can't expect me to not react to this news," I grind out.

Lucy's lip quivers as she takes a deep breath. And other than practically the entire town bearing witness as Susan stands between us, it's like déjà vu of the night Lucy walked out on me. Her struggling not to cry and me trying to reach her to understand what the hell is going on.

"Please. I only brought her back to Sunrise Bay on her doctor's suggestion to see if she would remember anything."

"Susan." My dad's deep voice comes from behind us. His large hand clasps me on the shoulder.

"Hank." The distaste Susan has for our family is clear as fucking crystal in her voice. She never liked me for her daughter, so there's no real surprise she's trying to keep me from her now.

"Let's find somewhere quiet and talk this out," Dad suggests. "We can head to the house—"

Susan raises her hand. "I'm taking Lucy back to Idaho tomorrow. I already apologized to Adam for disturbing your night."

"But—" I start.

My dad steps closer to Susan. "You cannot just expect Adam to go back to his life after this discovery. There are questions he needs the answers to."

I nod as though I'm that nineteen-year-old standing next to him again while he's on the phone with Susan and Lloyd Davis telling them to let Lucy and I marry.

"With all due respect, it wasn't your daughter who came running to you in tears a year ago. Obviously there's a reason their marriage didn't work out. If I was a lesser person, I'd say I told you so, Hank Greene."

"When was her accident?" I ask.

Susan shakes her head as though she's not going to entertain my questions.

"A little over three months ago," Lucy says. "First time ever on a horse, or so I'm told, and I got bucked off."

Susan sighs.

"Let the kids talk," my dad pleads with Susan.

She runs her hand over her face and inhales deeply. Glancing back, she looks at Lucy, then she steps closer to us, lowering her voice. "We were planning on staying in Anchorage, but I'll head over to Mandi's and get a room there for the night, assuming one is available. Lucy's really upset right now. I never expected her to have a breakthrough so fast, and it took us both by surprise. All the other memories she's gained have come in bits and pieces, slowly over days. Come by tomorrow morning and we'll talk once she's calmed down."

She can't be serious, but as I step to go around her again, my dad's hand lands on my arm to stop me.

"That's a good plan," Dad says.

I huff because I want to do this now.

"Let's say nine," Susan says, and my dad agrees. She turns around to join Lucy.

I clasp Susan's arm. "When you say breakthrough...?"

She pats Lucy's hand and Lucy's tears fall down her cheeks again.

"She didn't remember you until she saw you."

My dad sighs and I'm pretty sure my heart stops for a moment. I tried to strip Lucy out of my mind this past year. To erase her from my memory because it all hurt too much. But I can't imagine not remembering our history and all the good memories we shared. At the same time, I'm jealous that she doesn't have to bear the weight of what happened to us.

"We'll see you tomorrow," my dad says.

They walk away. My eyes lock with Lucy's as she looks over her shoulder until the crowd swallows them up.

Chapter Two

Lucy

$\mathcal{M}$om shuttles me away through the crowd. All I want to do is break free and run back to Adam—wrap my arms around his neck and allow him to pull me in, whisper to me that everything will be okay, that whatever happened to us isn't an issue anymore. Instead, I hide my tears as the townspeople we pass look and whisper about me. My mom huddles me into her chest as we make the short walk to the inn.

Suddenly, a memory flickers to life as if it was hidden in a dark room and Adam had the key to unlock the door and flip on the light for me.

WE WERE thirteen and it was his birthday.

Marla, his stepmom, threw him a huge party with balloons and streamers decorating the pergola outside by their pool. His dad was newly remarried, and the whole group of them had moved into the Greene family house on the hill about a year earlier.

I arrived with my best friend, Cora, while Adam was doing cannonball competitions with his friends, not paying any attention to the girls at the party. Then his brothers, Fisher and Xavier, and Fisher's friend, Cam, came out of the house. Most of the girls' mouths were ajar as they stripped off their shirts and did cannonballs that soaked everyone, including the bowls of chips near the pool.

Adam sat on the edge of the pool while his brothers razzed him and all the other boys about how the party was split down the middle with girls on one side and boys on the other. Then we played games I think Marla might have spurred. We did swimming contests and tag, and slowly all the girls and boys started interacting.

All the girls thought Adam was good-looking, and he was funny and sweet. Though I knew a lot of the girls liked him because he was a Greene. Every boy in his family had been a quarterback of the Sunrise Bay High School football team. Fisher was the captain and quarterback at the time, but rumor was Xavier would take over as the starting quarterback in his junior year because he was that good. It was expected that Adam would also play that position when he hit high school.

But I liked Adam because when Toby Turner depantsed me two years ago, earning me the nickname rainbow since my underwear had rainbows on them, Adam depantsed him back during the Christmas play in front of everyone. As Adam was being pulled away by Mrs. Fields, he winked at me. He got himself in a lot of trouble for getting payback for me.

"Chicken fights," Cam yelled, drawing me from remembering when I started to like Adam.

A lot had changed in two years. We'd all grown, and Adam's voice cracked from time to time. My breasts filled out my bikini, *and my hips had become wider after I got my period. I'd grown up with all those boys, yet we were all starting to see one another in a different light.*

"Go be Adam's partner." Cora elbowed me from the side of the pool.

I shook my head, kicking the water. "No."

"Stop playing from the sidelines. I know you like him."

Amara was already swimming toward Adam. I was jealous of the way she put herself out there. I pulled out my ponytail and repositioned it as though I couldn't be bothered.

Cora elbowed me again. "Luce, I know he likes you."

"No, you don't," I said, shaking my head.

"Everyone's known it since the depantsing of Toby Turner."

I loved Cora, but it'd been two years. Plus, Adam had been going through a rough time with his dad and Marla getting together. A lot had changed since then, so his attitude toward me probably had changed too.

Cam came over to us, pointing. "What about you two?"

Cameron Baker, heartthrob of Sunrise Bay, was standing in front of Cora and me. He was the starting running back and Fisher's right-hand man. If it wasn't for Hank Greene marrying his cousin's ex-wife, the Baker family might've taken the cake as the family everyone in Sunrise Bay respected most.

The Baker family ran the fishing piers. They were responsible for the livelihood of a lot of people in this town. But Cameron held a certain charismatic appeal. He was a natural flirt if you asked me. But he was no Adam Greene.

"You're Lucy Davis, right?" he asked.

Cora guffawed that he knew my name.

"Adam!" He snapped his finger and waved him over.

Adam swam over and I noticed how much wider his frame was than last summer.

"What?" he asked, never making eye contact with Cora or me.

"You and Lucy are gonna be partners," Cam said. "Come on and slide down in the water," he instructed me, as if I'd never done that before.

"You want me to get on his shoulders?" I asked, both praying Cameron wouldn't make me do this and at the same time wanting to.

"Cam." Adam shook his head, which kept my ass on the cement edge.

"Stop it. Come on. I'm doing you a huge favor."

"What?" Adam screeched and his voice turned high right at the end.

Cam patted him on the shoulder. "One day he won't sound like a frog anymore."

I think the reason people envied the Greenes was their big family. To an outsider, they all appeared to be close. Cameron Baker had been pulled into them, being Fisher's best friend. Having only a three-year-old brother, I would love to have siblings who had your back.

"Now stop playing games, let's go." He pointed at Cora. "You can be my partner."

"This is hardly fair. You're taller than me," Adam complained.

"True." Cam looked around. "Turner, get your ass over here."

Cora groaned. "I am not getting on Toby Turner's shoulders."

"Oh, come on," Cam implored.

Toby swam over. We'd made peace after the depantsing incident, and he and Adam actually became friends afterward.

We convinced Cora to get on Toby's shoulders, and once she was up in the water, Adam sank down into the water and I straddled his head with my legs hanging over his chest. His hands grabbed my shins and my body slowly emerged out of the water. I put my hands on his head and was surprised by how silky it was in my fingers.

"Okay, girls, on the count of three, you each have to try to get *the other one to fall off. Boys, stay strong." Cam leaned along the edge of the pool, Fisher and Xavier on either side of him, watching. "One. Two. Three."*

Adam and Toby walked toward one another, and Cora and I ended up laughing more than fighting, which aggravated the boys. My body wiggled, and Adam's hands on my bare skin were doing all sorts of things to my hormones. I was so preoccupied with his touch that Cora pushed me and I fell back, unable to keep my balance. As my body sank to the bottom, Adam's hands landed on my hips, guiding me back up. We both emerged from the water, staring at one another.

"I'm sorry," I said softly.

He shook out his hair. "Don't worry about it. You're okay?"

I nodded a few times. Our bodies were only inches apart and his hands were still on my hips. His gaze fell to my lips and it was as though the entire party disappeared and it was only us. I slid my tongue along my bottom lip because I read that your lips shouldn't be dry when you kiss a boy. He was so gorgeous, I lost all train of thought.

"Cake!" Mrs. Greene yelled, and everyone scrambled to get out of the pool.

Adam smiled and swam away, his hands falling off my body in a lingering way that suggested he didn't want to let me go.

That was when I knew Adam Greene and I were destined to be together. I even wrote it in my journal that night.

BEFORE WE REACH the doors of the inn, I stop, closing my eyes to make sure the memory is still there. I envision a younger Adam in his swim trunks, smiling at me. Yeah, it's still there.

"I had journals," I say.

"What, sweetie?" Mom opens the door.

She's been great the past three months, helping me try to remember. She didn't want to come back to Sunrise Bay though. Said that whatever made me leave a year ago was still here, and not knowing what it was, she thought returning could make things worse. But I pushed the issue until she worried I'd come by myself.

"I used to write in journals," I say again.

"You did?"

I nod. "You never had any at home?"

"You packed up your room when you..." She heads toward the reception desk where a young man I don't recognize stands, her words trailing off like she wasn't speaking.

Once we've secured a room for the night and we're inside, I sit on the bed. "Mom."

She's busy taking off her coat and getting out of her shoes, checking her phone as if I didn't say her name. I'm just realizing that she never told me about Adam or even the fact that I was married. How could she keep that from me?

"Mom," I say again.

"What, sweetie? I never saw any journals." She's talking to her phone.

"Will you please look at me?"

She glances up.

"Can we talk about what a huge thing this is? I just remembered being at Adam's thirteenth birthday party. I mean, until twenty minutes ago, I didn't even know he existed."

She puts her phone down and sits on the edge of the bed, taking my hands. "This is what I was afraid of. I'm not going to lie, I'd hoped maybe you wouldn't remember being married. When you came to us in Idaho, you were so distraught. You didn't get out of bed for an entire month."

"Why did we break up?"

She shakes her head. "I don't know. You wouldn't say."

"Why? Why wouldn't I have told you?" My forehead creases.

She sighs, her telltale sign she's holding back information and would rather not tell me. "I think you were afraid I would say I told you so."

"Why would you have done that?"

"Because we forbade your marriage." She pats my hand. "I never saw you get married, Luce. Your father and I didn't agree with it and there was a fight and..."

I slide my hands out from hers and stand, looking out the window that has views of the bay. "Why didn't you support us?"

She sighs again. It's grating on my nerves. "It's a long story."

"Good thing we have nowhere to be then."

She stands and grabs her overnight bag, ready to go to the bathroom.

"Mom," I plead, "you can't keep me in the dark. Dr. Lipstein said when I have questions, you should answer them and maybe they'll help me remember."

At times in the past three months, I've felt my mom keeping information from me. My brother, Zane, would say something that didn't quite make sense to me and then my parents would shift conversation in another direction.

"Some things are meant to stay in the past. You came back to us. Can't we just let that be?"

I raise my hands in frustration. What did she expect to happen when we returned here? Did she hope I would remember nothing and this entire part of my life would be erased forever? I think I'm starting to understand why she was so hesitant for me to return.

"Either you tell me or I hear it from Adam, because I'm

not leaving Sunrise Bay without an answer." I cross my arms.

"Okay, okay. Just let me get ready for bed and process everything, then we'll hash out what happened." She opens the door and disappears down the hall.

I wait for the bathroom door to shut down the hall, then I grab my coat and slide out of the room. If she has to think about it, she won't tell me the full truth. And I'm starting to figure out that it's up to me to remember for myself.

Going downstairs, I tiptoe past the front desk and out the door, but I freeze in place when I see Mandi's finger poking Adam in the chest.

"What's going on?" I ask.

Both of them look over. Adam steps forward only for Mandi to wrap her hand around his wrist and tug him back.

Looks like it's not only my family who wants to keep us apart.

Chapter Three

Adam

Mandi's hand is so tight around my wrist, she's going to pop open a vein with her nails.

Lucy stops outside the doors to the inn.

My stepsister Mandi owns this place and I'm assuming she was appointed the designated Greene to watch out for me showing up here because as soon as my truck pulled into the parking lot, she was out the door, telling me to go home.

How can I go home? I drove Alicia home and she tried to lure me into her house by palming my dick through my pants. Sadly, nothing happened, not even a chub—the consequences of having your estranged wife show back up in town is limp dick apparently. So I walked her to the door and said good night.

I told myself to drive home. I really did. To just go to bed. But I couldn't convince myself I'd get any sleep. Still, waiting until tomorrow, like my dad said, is good advice. But somehow, my truck took a wrong turn and then another wrong turn, leaving me outside the inn.

"Hey, Luce," Mandi says, still with a vise grip on my wrist. Seriously, her hands are freakishly strong. "Did you need something?"

Lucy shakes her head, our gazes finding one another under the dim lights of the parking lot. "No. Just thought I'd clear my head."

"Where's your mom?" Mandi asks.

"Getting ready for bed." Lucy zips up her jacket and shuffles her feet in place. "Adam, do you want to talk?" Her voice is so shaky and raspy, I barely recognize it.

I dislodge myself from Mandi's Herculean grip and walk toward her. "Sure."

"Adam..." Mandi's tone holds warning, but I raise my hand.

"It's my life."

She says nothing else, and Lucy smiles over my shoulder at what was once one of her good friends. Mandi's only a year older than us, and when Lucy and I were dating in high school, it was usually Lucy, Mandi, Chevelle, and me hanging out in the basement of our parents' house. I wonder if Lucy remembers that.

"Please don't make me the one responsible for organizing a search party, okay? Don't run off," Mandi says to our retreating backs.

"Don't worry. I'll bring her back within an hour," I say.

"An hour?" Mandi screeches.

But I'm too busy soaking in the fact I'm walking toward the bay with Lucy next to me. It's been so long since I've seen her, so it's odd how normal yet weird it feels to be near her.

Lucy is taking in everything as we increase our distance from any sign of life.

With tourist season starting tomorrow, our small town of Sunrise Bay is more crowded than normal. Luckily, down by the inn, it's more secluded. The majority of guests staying at the inn are probably having fun in the square, where most of the festivities are tonight. I find us a spot on the rocks closer to the shoreline and we sit. I pick up small pebbles and toss them in, needing to keep my hands busy before I do something stupid like touch her.

I'm not sure what to say, so like an idiot I blurt, "If I'm dead tomorrow, your mom probably killed me."

"I get the gist she isn't a fan?" Lucy sits next to me, picking up her own pebbles and throwing them in the water.

I glance over. The moonlight shines down on her face, reminding me of the nights in our cabin up in the mountains when we'd look at the stars and end up making love on our deck. I shut my eyes because that no longer exists. We aren't that naive couple who thinks love can conquer the world anymore. In fact, now I know for certain it can't.

"What do you remember?" I ask her.

I know absolutely nothing about amnesia, other than what I've seen in the movies, and I'm pretty sure that's not completely accurate. Like that rom-com Lucy made me watch once where the guy is in a coma and when he wakes up, they convince him he has a fiancée. But whoops, she fell in love with the brother while he was fighting for his life.

"At first nothing. I didn't know my name. But the doctors called my parents, and as soon as I saw them, I remembered them. They thought my memory issues would be temporary, but then nothing else came for a long time."

"So you forgot all about me, huh?"

"I guess," she says. "I remembered they were my parents, but I couldn't recollect much else. Then when I saw you, I remembered you're my husband."

"Soon-to-be *ex*-husband." I mentally reprimand myself for my tone when her shoulders sink.

"Can I ask you what happened between us? Did we break up because of your girlfriend?"

I guffaw. Of course I must be the one at fault. Anger is a hot pit in my stomach, but it's still hard to admit one of the most embarrassing and painful things that's ever happened to me. "I was never unfaithful to you. *You* left *me*."

Her forehead wrinkles. "Why?"

What did I do in my life to deserve this torture? To have to relive all this shit again just as I was starting to feel like I could move past it. I stare at the water, at some of the fishing vessels there. I'd like to dive in and ask them to take me with them out to sea for months.

I shrug, trying to appear unaffected. "You said you wanted to live your life. That you weren't happy anymore."

"Oh." Her voice is meek and weary.

I want to curse myself for the instinct that wants to fix what's troubling her. That's something a husband does, not a soon-to-be ex-husband.

Too antsy to sit, I stand and head closer to the shoreline. The sky is dark, the stars overfilling the sky. A romantic scene for some maybe, but not for us. Those days are long gone.

"How come when I saw you, none of that came back? For a moment there, I was so happy." She pulls her knees up to her chest and rests her chin on them, staring at the water.

"I'm sure all the reasons for your unhappiness will come back to you," I say in a derisive tone. Which is the exact reason I'll be keeping my distance. Otherwise I'll get close to her again, just for her to sweep the rug out from under me once she remembers. Then I'll be back to pulling myself up from the depths of despair and I can't do it again.

"On the way back to the inn, I remembered your thirteenth birthday party."

I glance back at her and she has a soft smile on her lips. I remember it was the first time I ever touched her. I fucking loved Cam for suggesting a chicken fight that day. "I wished for you to be my girlfriend when I blew out the candles that day."

She sucks in a breath and I wish I would've kept that to myself. I'm not sure if I ever told Lucy that before or not. "Really?"

"That was over a decade ago. First crushes and all that shit." I throw a rock out and it sinks into the water. My heart feels a kinship with it.

"You always had a great arm," she says.

I nod. "So that's all you remember, huh? That I was your husband, at thirteen you went to my birthday party, and I have a great arm?" I head back to the rocks.

"So far. I'm sorry."

"What are you sorry for?"

"I can tell my appearance bothers you. That I've upset you."

I blow out a breath.

"What?" Her legs drop and she reaches out but retracts her hand immediately. "I'm upsetting you?"

I shake my head. "It's just weird... you don't remember much about me other than that I'm your husband, but you can still read my body language."

"Yeah, that is weird, I guess. My doctor said it's different for everyone. He pushed for me to come here, but my mom wasn't very receptive to the idea. I'm starting to understand why."

The last thing I want to discuss right now are her parents. I'm not the person to fill in her missing pieces. Welcoming her and helping her might be the right thing to do, but it's not my place. Not anymore. "Why's that?"

"My mom said she didn't come to our wedding?"

I huff that even while Lucy is sick, Susan is trying to turn her away from us—from me.

"What? What am I missing?" Lucy asks.

My head falls back. "It's her job to tell you, not mine."

"Seriously?"

Her voice raises and it throws me off at first. Hell, sure we had our fights, but Lucy was a second grade teacher and she rarely lost her temper or ever raised her voice. I always said she had the most patience of anyone I ever met.

"Do you have any idea what it's like to not know anything?" She rises up from the rocks and walks back toward the inn. "I thought we shared something. That you'd tell me. You are my husband."

"Was!" I yell. "I *was* your husband until you walked out on me. I'm sorry you got flung from a horse and can't remember that, but do you have any idea what I've been through this past year? The love of my life left me without anything more than a 'you just don't make me happy anymore.'"

Her shoulders fall and she slowly pivots around to face me. "I don't remember any of that."

"It doesn't mean it didn't happen."

She crouches and buries her head in her hands. "You hate me!"

Fuck me. My jaw tenses and my fists clench at my sides. "I don't hate you. I—"

"*Lucy!*" Susan screams from the balcony of the inn, then rushes down the stairs toward us.

"Fucking hell," I murmur.

Lucy's head flies up. "So you hate her too?"

I shake my head and don't answer because Lucy doesn't remember the hell they put her through. All she must remember are her parents from when she was younger. I'm sure not going to be the one to help her figure this out.

"You can't just take her like that," Susan says when she reaches us, trying to catch her breath.

Mandi is right behind her, along with my stepbrother Jed. He sighs and gives me that look to say this sucks.

Yeah, tell me about it.

"I didn't take her," I grind out.

"You expect me to believe that? You have a new girlfriend, why don't you just keep moving on?"

Lucy stands, and her mom wraps her arm around Lucy's shoulders.

"Susan, you're being unfair," Mandi says. "I was there. Lucy wanted to talk to Adam."

"I did, Mom," Lucy says.

I blow out a breath and run my hand through my hair, pulling at my neck to relieve the tension building there.

Susan ignores Lucy's comment. "Come on, sweetie. Let's get you inside."

"She's not ten," I say.

Jed groans.

Mandi sighs.

Susan stops and turns around. "Your animosity toward me isn't going to help her."

"Maybe a call from Idaho would've been helpful."

"Okay, let's go." Jed puts his arm around my shoulders, as if I'm drunk or something.

"Listen to your stepbrother, Adam. We'll see you tomorrow morning." She walks away, Lucy's eyes filled with questions.

Once they're gone, I sit down and lean back, staring at the sky and wondering how the fuck I got here. Jed falls down next to me and Mandi follows. No one says anything. They don't give me advice or tell me what to do. They just lie there and let me collect my thoughts.

How can Susan Davis find our family so despicable? We're there for one another all the damn time, which is more than I can say for her.

Chapter Four

Lucy

My mom is still fast asleep when I slip out of our room at the inn. This time I left her a note and told her I'd have my cell phone on me. For the past two months, I've tried to keep up running since it clears my head and allows all the pressure of remembering anything to disappear.

Thankfully, Mandi isn't at the reservation desk. I'm pretty sure the guy who is there knows who I am though, due to his furrowed brow when I wave and walk out the doors. At least in Idaho, I didn't always feel like everyone knew more about me than I did. Was I nice to the guy or were we childhood enemies? Who knows?

I put in my earbuds, scroll through my running app, and turn on my music. I'm in this whole grunge music phase. My mom says she doesn't remember what kind of music I listened to, but she doesn't think it was this dark. I'd like to ask Adam, because I think he'd know, but he doesn't seem too willing to share information with me.

I start off on my run, hoping I don't get lost in the woods and eaten by a bear. I'm not sure how much time passes, but I'm running up a hill, about to cross over a two-lane road to continue on the wooden trail, so I slow to a standing jog and look both ways. There's a slight hill to the right. I'm about to step on the pavement to cross when a Cadillac whizzing by makes me backstep. All I see is white and blue hair through the windows. I shake my head and jog across the street, hoping to get back into the zone again.

The Cadillac's wheels screech to a halt, the back fish-tailing slightly. I glance over my shoulder, pulling my earbuds from my ears to see if something happened or if I need to sprint for my life because it's an ax murderer.

"I spilled my coffee!" a woman yells.

The car door opens, and I take my cell phone out of the side of my leggings, prepared to call the police. My thumb hovers over the nine.

My fear relaxes when Ethel, Adam's grandmother, climbs out of the Cadillac. Not only is it nice to see her, but it's nice to know who she is as soon as I do.

"It's all over me!" the other woman yells.

"Relax, I'll get you another one." Ethel shakes her head.

"My car or my clothes?"

"Shh, you old bat, my granddaughter's returned to town." Ethel opens her arms and crosses the street boldly, as though the oncoming cars will just stop for her. "Lucy!" She hugs me. "Oh, my Lucy. I heard a rumor you were back. Figures the one year I miss the night before tourist day. The struggles of getting old." She leans in and covers her mouth. "Constipation is a bitch."

"Good to know," I say, hugging her back, thankful that I remember her.

"I knew you couldn't forget me."

I laugh. "It's good to see you, Mrs. Greene."

"I'm hard to forget." She winds her arm through mine, walking us back to the car. "Come on. Dori and I are headed into town to celebrate tourist day."

I stop in the middle of the road and slide my arm back out of hers as politely as I can. "I'm not ready for all that commotion just yet."

"Oh, completely understandable."

The passenger side door opens, and a blue-haired woman gets out. I feel as though I should know her.

"Lucy," she says. "How nice to see you."

"Thank you." I smile.

"I'm Dori. You know, I have a granddaughter-in-law who's a doctor. You should go see her. She's brilliant."

"She's a family doctor, Dori, not a head doctor," Ethel says.

"Don't knock Stella. She has more of a degree than you have," Dori says.

These two are something else.

"Sorry, Dori's in a bad mood," Ethel says to me.

"I wasn't in a bad mood until you spilled coffee all over me." She looks down at her pants that match the blue in her floral shirt. The outfit seems to pull the blue in her hair out more.

"Because I saw Lucy." Ethel smiles brightly at me. Maybe she'll explain to me the whole situation between my mom and Adam.

Shit. I look at my phone. It's eight-thirty. I've been running for well over an hour. As though my mom feels my panic, her name flashes on my screen as my phone vibrates.

"I have to go. It was very nice seeing you again," I say

before hugging Ethel and smiling at Dori. I've decided I'm not pretending to know someone if I don't anymore. It's weird to hug people when we both know I have no clue who they are.

"Are you okay?" Ethel asks, and I step backward a few feet.

"Great, I just have to finish my run and get back to my mom at the inn."

"We can drive you," Dori suggests.

I raise my hand to say that's okay. I turn around to head into the woods when a semi crosses over the hill and blares his horn when he sees me in the road. I stand there as if I'm made of stone.

"*Lucy*! Get out of the street!" Ethel screams.

I look over at her and snap out of it, dashing to the side of the road. But I'm not on the trail, and I fall down into a ditch that's all muddy from the recent snowmelt. The semi passes by with a whoosh and I lie back, not wanting to get up out of sheer embarrassment.

The two old women peer over the edge of the road at me.

"Do you not remember that semis can squish you like a pancake?" Dori asks.

I sit up, looking at my clothes, now caked in mud. My phone vibrates again. "Yes, I do remember. It just took me by surprise."

Honestly, I wish I had an answer to why I froze just now. As sad as it is, I've wondered if I hit my head again, would my memory resurface? I know, stupid, but late at night when I'm trying so hard I give myself a migraine, I fear I'll never be who I was.

"I should call Adam," Ethel says.

"*No!*" I yell and climb up from the ditch.

"Well, we're at least taking you with us," Ethel says.

I can't refuse their offer now.

Of course, these veteran mothers are prepared with towels in the back of the car. I don't ask why though. They lay them out for me and I slide into the back seat, relieved to at least have a ride back to the inn.

Until Ethel slams her foot on the gas and my head hits the back of the seat.

Dori peers over the passenger seat. "You remember me now?"

I shake my head.

"Didn't think so." She turns forward and I send a text to my mom, saying I'll be there shortly.

> It's fine. I packed my bags. Please pack yours. I'm going to meet Adam and his father for coffee and then we'll leave.

My stomach sinks while I stare at the text message. She can't be serious. Adam was my first breakthrough in weeks. I hammer out a message.

> No. Please wait. I'm coming and then I'll go with you.

> *Sweetie, it's 8:45 now, I don't want to be late.*

> *Call them and ask to push it back.*

> *Truth is, it's better if you just don't go. Let me handle this. You had a tough day yesterday.*

I clench my phone. She's going to leave me out of this,

and now I've fallen in mud and have to shower before I can join them. I don't like all these people making decisions on my behalf.

"Take me to town," I say to Ethel.

Ethel glances at Dori. It's clear they're having some weird conversation with just their eyebrows.

"Sure," Ethel says. "Anywhere specific?"

"Where people would meet for coffee?"

"That's vague," Dori says but looks back at me. "Do you remember what coffee is?"

I stare at her blankly. "Yes, I know what coffee is. I just need to find my mom, Adam, and Mr. Greene."

"Oh," Ethel says and her and Dori's eyebrows go in all different directions. "Why?"

"Because this is my life and so what if I don't remember anything? I'm going to eventually. One day I'll find out exactly why my mom and Adam don't like one another, why I'd leave Adam and go to my parents, and everything else about who Lucy Davis was. Or is."

"You mean Lucy Greene," Dori says.

Shit. I never thought about that. I am Lucy Greene, but only until Adam divorces me.

We pull into downtown and I reposition my ponytail, trying to look halfway presentable.

As I step out of the Cadillac in the parking lot behind the square, a minivan pulls up beside the car and a woman flies out, swarming me. "Lucy, Lucy!"

My back presses against the car as she tackles me and hugs me so tightly, I struggle to breathe. Pulling back, she holds my forearms, looking me over.

Then her face transforms into a scowl and her pointer finger is right in front of my face. "You leave me again and so help me God, I will sucker punch you right between the legs."

I squeeze my thighs together on instinct, but the only thing I'm happy about is that I recognize her. "Cora."

She's a little older than I remember, but her strawberry-blonde hair and freckled face still holds youthfulness.

"She remembers her, but not me?" Dori says from next to us.

"Hello, Ethel. Dori." Cora tips her head in greeting. A crying baby sounds from the minivan and Cora backs up. "Sorry, give me a moment." She pulls out a baby and settles it on her hip.

"You have a baby?"

Her smile dims.

I hate that reaction. As though I'm disappointing people.

"Yeah, Luce, I married Toby, remember? And I was pregnant when you left."

My heart sinks. I don't remember such milestones in one of my best friend's lives. But I do know that there was never a thing I kept from Cora, so maybe she can help me regain some of my memories.

"Can we talk in a bit? Are you busy?" I ask.

"It's story time at the bookstore. It's Brody's favorite time of day. But after, you can come over while he takes a nap?"

"You should go to story time with them," Ethel says.

"Next time. I have to get to the coffee shop."

"Just go in for a second. In the meantime, I'll find Hank and Adam for you." Ethel pulls out her cell phone.

Cora's already got her stroller out and is placing her son inside. "Walk with me. You were gone last night before I could catch up with you. We arrived a half hour after the action, from what I heard."

We round the corner into the town square and it's just

like last night but not nearly as crowded. Cora stops in front of a bookstore next to the brewery. I look inside.

"Presley?" I ask, remembering the woman inside from last night.

"You know her?" Cora acts surprised.

"I met her last night. She looks so much like Clara."

"Oh yeah. That's a whole thing I'll have to fill you in on when we catch up."

"So Cade, huh?"

She nods. "She just whirled into town and put a sold sign on the man. Another Greene off the market." Her smile dims again.

I want to say 'stop it. I'm fine. Don't feel sorry for me.'

"Of course, you were the first to get a Greene man off the market," she says, elbowing me.

"And from what I hear, I was the first one to put a Greene back on the market as well."

She puts her arm around my shoulders. "Don't worry, you're totally going to win him back. That Alicia is nobody."

Another mother walks past us into the bookstore, and we hear Presley announce that story time is starting.

"Oh, I have to go. Here." Cora pulls out her phone and hands it to me. "Call yourself and then I'll call you afterward. Give you the address to my place."

I do what she says, and she hugs me one more time before rushing inside. I think about her words. Win him back? Is that something I want to do? I wish I could answer that, but until I regain my memory of why I left him in the first place, I'm not sure I can. Right now, I feel as though a huge chunk of my heart has been dug out with a dull shovel. But past me must've had reasons for leaving my husband, right?

And then I spot my mom across the street. I'm about to follow her until she gets into a truck and drives away.

I know that truck. It's Adam's.

"I guess you weren't invited," Dori says.

The old bat is right. As if not remembering that it's my life, two people I love are purposely keeping me out of every decision that affects me.

Chapter Five

Adam

Not everyone in Sunrise Bay loves our family. We live in a small town where most people know one another. Because my grandfather bought a prominent parcel of land up on a hill overlooking the square years ago and built himself a house, most people think we're a helluva lot richer than we are.

My grandfather was an honest man. Sadly, his brother wasn't. But some people, like Susan Davis, decided early on which of the Greene brothers they sided with. Since Susan's dad worked alongside my grandfather's brother, and he was responsible for her family's livelihood, Susan's always loved him and hated my grandfather. It's stupid shit that should mean nothing in the present, since my grandfather is long dead and his brother lives in Arizona. But as my dad says, you can't change people's thinking. You can try to enlighten them, but that's about all.

We sit down at a diner in Lake Starlight, Lard Have Mercy. I used to come here quite a bit after my mom died.

My dad wanted to flee the sympathetic looks in Sunrise Bay.

Susan picks up a menu and looks out into the square and the gazebo. Lake Starlight has a Founder's Day Parade every year, and from the number of trucks hanging up banners, it looks like they're setting up for it.

"Sunrise Bay is so much prettier," Susan remarks.

I slide in next to my dad. "Rylan's soccer coach lives here. He's married to a Bailey."

Susan nods as though she doesn't know who they are. We all know the Baileys. The nine Bailey siblings lost their parents tragically when they were younger, leaving the oldest siblings to take custody of the rest. When tragic things like that happen, word of it carries over to nearby towns, especially with our three small towns clustered together—Lake Starlight, Sunrise Bay, and Greywall.

"Thanks for understanding that I wanted to go outside of Sunrise Bay. The eyes and ears there are just waiting for gossip, and I didn't want Lucy here during this conversation."

"We shouldn't be keeping things from her," I say.

My dad raises his coffee mug for the waitress, and she comes by and fills the cups. That's his signal for me to shut up. "Susan, I understand you wanting to protect Lucy. She's your daughter. But she's also an adult. An adult who's married to Adam. If we wanted to be technical here..."

Susan's jaw shifts left and right. "Just spit it out, Hank."

Surely he's not thinking I'm going to take Lucy back? Fuck that. Only for her memory to resurface after I've grown close to her, and then I'm back to where I started a year ago?

"You said Adam was a breakthrough for her," Dad says. "Why not give her more time here? See if more resurfaces for her."

I choke on my coffee but manage to swallow it.

"Do you have any idea how much work I've missed since her accident? I'm not tenured at the university yet, so my job is hanging on by a thread." She stirs her coffee. "And after last night, I'm not sure it is the right place for her."

"Last night?" My dad glances my way through the corner of his eyes.

"So the Greenes don't share everything with one another, huh?" She huffs, her narrowed eyes pointed at me.

"I went to the inn," I admit.

My father's shoulders sink. "I told you not to."

If he thinks I'm going to apologize, he's crazy. I have so many questions and I don't trust Susan to answer them. "She's my wife."

"That's not what you said last night," Susan taunts me like a child.

"We were in an argument. Don't act like you understand our situation."

My dad places his hand on my arm to quiet me. The waitress must be used to family drama because she reappears with a smile, pen poised over her notepad, asking what she can get us.

"Just a muffin," Susan says.

My dad says he's just having coffee.

"I'll have an omelet with cheese and bacon. Hash browns, crispy, and another side of bacon."

The waitress jots it down, smiles, and walks away.

"One day you'll have to change your eating habits."

Susan offers advice I don't want, so I say nothing since the man who taught me not to say anything if I didn't have anything nice to say is sitting right next to me. Hate for him to think I don't take any of his fatherly advice.

"As I was saying, my bag is already packed and if Lucy

does as I asked, she should be at the inn, waiting for my return with her own bags packed. This was never more than a quick trip in and out." Susan pretends like she's so proper with her chin tilted up, gazing down at us. As if we're having tea with lemon wedges and shortbread cookies at high noon. She always thought she was hot shit because she was a professor. Someone needs to remind her that Anchorage College and Harvard aren't exactly the same. Not that I'm bashing my alma mater.

"Marla and I would be happy to have Lucy stay with us."

Again I choke on my coffee. Why does Dad throw this shit out there right as I take a drink? I bet he's doing it on purpose since I went against his wishes last night.

"Yeah, um, no." She pours another artificial sugar in her cup, the spoon stirring constantly. All I want to do is take the spoon out of her cup and fling it across the room. "She'll come back to Idaho with me."

"Are you sure you don't just want her to forget her life here? Forget Adam?" my dad asks in a sterner voice.

I could probably sneak out of this conversation. The kids playing over at the gazebo are having way more fun than me.

"Whatever happened that your son is being so tight-lipped about is the reason she left. They were over before the accident." Susan continues to stir her coffee.

"All she said was she wasn't happy," I chime in.

Susan says nothing and rolls her eyes as though she doesn't believe me. "Convenient that you're already seeing someone."

I slide out of the booth to leave before my anger gets the better of me, but I stand at the end of the table, unable to keep the words inside. "Alicia and I are a new thing, and it isn't serious. I've had the year from hell without your daughter in my life. I don't want to share that with you, but I will so you'll stop assuming this is my fault. She walked out on me. I didn't cheat on her, I didn't hit her, I didn't lie to her. There was no reason for her to leave me, but she did. Now she's back in town, not even remembering why she decided to walk out on our marriage. If you want to let all those memories stay hidden, for her never to become the Lucy we all love, then shame on you, Susan."

She leans back, gaping at my dad as though he should put me over his knee and spank me. "Are you honestly questioning my intentions for Lucy's recovery?"

I huff. "I'm questioning your intentions of making sure Lucy remembers *every* part of her past. Maybe your hatred for our family has twisted your decision-making ability."

"Adam." My dad clears his throat, but before he can add another word, I continue.

"Let's be honest, Susan. You're afraid I can worm myself into your daughter's heart again. Then if she doesn't remember why she left me, there's a good chance we might get back together and that'd be your worst nightmare. Even if I was the one who took care of your daughter, loved her with my entire heart, and you were the one who chose not to come to our wedding and wrote her off."

"Adam," my dad says again.

I lean in over the table, lowering my voice, thankful we're not in Sunrise Bay. "But you don't have to worry because losing Lucy made me feel dead inside. I never want to feel that pain again. It was like someone put my heart through a meat grinder. So stick around and give her memory a chance to come back, but you don't have to worry, I'm never going to love Lucy, or any other woman, ever again."

I storm out of the diner, the bell chiming as my goodbye.

Since I drove us all, I head to the Lake Starlight gazebo and sit my ass down on a bench, waiting until they're ready to leave, which I hope is soon.

A girl kicking a soccer ball around with her brother looks at me. "Hey, you're Rylan's brother, right?"

I huff. "Calista Bailey," I say, recognizing her. She and Rylan are coached by the same instructor.

She looks around. "Is he here?"

I shake my head, watching her footwork that's so much like Rylan's. You never see my kid brother without a soccer ball, and from the few times I've witnessed these two together in lessons, she and Rylan are evenly matched.

"Why are you here?" Calista asks.

A boy comes by and kicks the ball out from her feet.

"*Dion!*" she yells.

I nod toward the diner. "Breakfast."

"That's my dad's place." Calista points at the maroon awning with gold lettering that reads Terra and Mare. It's the fanciest place in Lake Starlight, so it's usually a special occasion or a date if you go there. "He's not open for breakfast though."

I nod. "He's a great chef. I've eaten there."

The Dion kid kicks the ball, and it hits Calista in the ass. She runs off after him, irritated.

"I'll tell Rylan you said hello," I say to her retreating back.

She stops and turns around. "I didn't tell you to do that."

"I thought you guys were friends?"

Her forehead wrinkles. "I am not friends with Rylan Greene."

I hold up my hands and chuckle. "Okay then, I won't mention even seeing you."

"Good."

She kicks the ball to her brother as a man comes out of Terra and Mare. He jogs across the street and steals the ball. I recognize him as the chef from Terra and Mare, so he must be Calista's dad.

"Adam!" my dad yells across the lawn.

I stand, meeting him and Susan at my truck. She sits next to me, and the twenty-minute drive back to the inn is uncomfortable and awkward. Pulling up to the inn, I'm happy she says nothing to me as she opens her door to climb out. There was a time in my relationship with Lucy when I wanted Susan and Lloyd Davis to welcome me into their family. I tried hard to get them to approve of me. Those days are gone now.

I'm about to reverse out of the parking spot when a Cadillac pulls up and blocks me in. My grandma is in the driver's seat, her friend Dori in the passenger seat. To my surprise, Lucy steps out of the back, covered in mud, and starts toward Susan, not looking happy.

So with a sigh, I put the truck in park and climb out, along with my dad. Will my life ever be normal? I'm thinking not, at this point. Who else can say their estranged wife returns to them with no memory of leaving?

Add on the fact that I lied to Susan in that diner. I never stopped loving Lucy, but the hell if anyone in this town will ever know.

Chapter Six

Lucy

Pulling into the inn and seeing my mom walking away from Adam's truck spurs the anger that diminished during my breakfast with Ethel and Dori at Two Brothers and an Egg. I slam the car door and Mom turns around.

"You were supposed to be packing," she says. "What happened to you?" She steps toward me, but I put up my hand to stop her.

"She slipped down a hill," Dori says, running her hand down my arm as if we're old friends. I still don't remember her, even after she quizzed me during my pancake breakfast while the rest of the people at the diner whispered and pointed at me.

"When? Where?" My mom's gaze falls down my body as though she's a doctor and could see if something was actually wrong.

"I just lost my footing," I say, brushing her off.

The door of the inn opens and Mandi steps out, her red

hair pulled into a ponytail higher up on her head. She walks over to Adam and Hank, who I hadn't yet realized are here. The three of them watch the scene unfold. Adam's hands are stuffed into his pockets and he's rocking back on his heels.

I get distracted from looking at him by someone snapping their fingers in front of my face.

My mom.

"This is why you can't go running in an area you aren't familiar with. Come on, we're going to pack and then we're leaving." My mom tugs on my arm, but I pry it out of her grasp.

"Just let her be, Susan," Ethel says.

My mom stops and turns toward the Greenes. "Do you people have anything other to do than to bother us? She's not your family anymore."

"Susan," Ethel says in that tone like everyone is family in Sunrise Bay.

"No, Ethel. The last person I need a lecture from is you."

Dori steps closer to my mom. "What's that supposed to mean?"

"Let her be, she's always been a stubborn one." Ethel crosses her arms.

"Please, you people act like you're all holier-than-thou, when in reality, your entire family started out taking what's other's."

"Mom," I say.

Ethel shakes her head and smiles at me. "Let her speak her piece. It's been a long time coming, right, Susan? So let's get it all out in the open. Maybe it will spur some memories for Lucy."

Mom huffs and sighs as though she's about to throw a tantrum. "I am not going to sit here and rehash history when it doesn't even matter. I'm taking Lucy home."

"This is her home," Adam says, stepping away from his family.

Even knowing something must've happened to make me leave him, I can't help the way my heart flutters at his declaration.

"Not anymore," Mom says. "You aren't part of her life."

"She views me as her husband still, and I'd like to help her find her memories." He briefly looks at me but turns away as our eyes meet.

"What?" My mom appears surprised.

"Listen to the boy," Ethel says.

I catch a proud smile on Hank's face.

"Your mom doesn't like my family, Luce... y. Years ago, my grandma"—he motions to Ethel—"found herself torn between two brothers and she chose my grandfather. Some people feel as though my grandma did something bad by following her heart. Then when my dad married his cousin's ex-wife, Marla, some people saw the entire thing happening all over again since Marla used to be married to my grandfather's brother's son. Your mom is one of those people."

Jeez, I feel as though someone needs to draw me a detailed family tree.

A flash of a memory comes to mind. My mom standing over me at the kitchen table, telling me I couldn't go to prom. That the Greene family I was spending time with didn't care about people's feelings. They were selfish and one day Adam would break my heart.

My head slowly raises, and my breath weighs heavy in my chest at the realization why my mom did everything she could to keep me from coming to Sunrise Bay.

"You," I say, not even really sure if I'm referring to Adam or my mom.

Adam glances back at Hank and he nods, hiding a small smile.

My mom points at herself. "What? Did you remember something?"

I swallow past the dry lump in my throat. "You hate him," I say more to myself than her. "That's why."

She puts her hand on my arm, but I shrug off her touch.

"You were purposely trying to keep me from remembering Adam." I step back.

"No. That's not it." She looks over her shoulder. "This is ridiculous. Your family thinks they own this town because there's so many of you." She turns back my way.

This entire time, I trusted her. I trusted that she wanted what I wanted. To remember who I was and to get back to being that person. But then all the doctor's visits flash in my head. The ones where she said it would be okay, that we'd try to get my memories back, but if I couldn't, I could still live a fulfilling life, meet someone.

"You were trying to hide me," I say. My heart races and I bend forward to catch my breath.

"Lucy," my mom says.

I shake my head. "Don't talk to me." I stand up straight and walk by her toward Adam. He steps back at my approach. My stomach knots, hating where we're at. "Tell me more."

He shrugs. "There isn't much else to say. She was never okay with us, and because of that, your family wasn't at our wedding."

"I wasn't..." My hand hovers over my stomach. "Pregnant?"

"No." His gaze falls to my mom over my shoulder, speaking directly to her. "We married out of love..." His gaze shifts back to me. "At least I thought we did."

"And they couldn't accept that?"

He shakes his head.

"Stop listening to them." My mom comes up behind me.

"Why?" I yell and turn around. "He's the only one who's telling me anything. He's the one who keeps spurring new memories for me. Not like you, who's hiding things from me, hiding my past because you didn't approve of us. This is my life."

"We're going back to Idaho, let's go." She tries for my arm again, and again I yank it out of her hold.

"I'm not going anywhere," I say.

Mom sighs. "And where will you go, Lucy? You have no job, no money."

"This is where I need to be." I have tears in my eyes.

"You need to be with people you can trust." She holds out her hand, and I back away from her. "You're being foolish. All he wants is for you to come back so he can break your heart again. You don't even know what happened to make you leave. You probably found out some secret, since all of them have one, and left him."

"Stop!" Ethel screams, stepping between my mom and me. "Enough about my family. Do you understand me?"

My eyes grow wide, but my mom's stance grows more agitated.

"Did I have a history with both the Greene brothers? I did. But I loved my husband, and we made a family together. Let's remember that Jeff Greene ruined his marriage all on his own before Hank was even in the picture." She turns around. "Sorry, Mandi."

Mandi shakes her head and waves it off.

"He didn't appreciate Marla and didn't honor their marriage," Ethel says. "So please step down from the high horse you're on and look around. These two kids fell in love a long time ago. Now I don't know what made Lucy leave. Unfortunately, we might never find out, but they both deserve to do everything in their power to bring back that memory and find peace. But if I hear one more bad word about my family out of your mouth, you will be sorry."

"Yeah, she will," Dori says.

"Dori." Hank shakes his head, but he and Mandi snicker.

Mom throws her hands in the air. "I'm so over this place. Let's go, Lucy."

"I'm not going," I say to her retreating back. She stops at the inn's door and turns around. "I have to stay here and figure this out."

"Suit yourself," she says and storms into the inn.

Everyone is quiet for a moment, and the realization of what I just decided hits me.

"Ethel, Dori, Hank, the restaurant is trying out a new cinnamon roll recipe. Want to give me your opinion?" Mandi asks.

"Yeah," Hank says.

"I do love my sweets," Ethel says.

"Try and keep me away from those cinnamon rolls," Dori says.

They disappear inside the restaurant attached to the inn.

"Thank you," I say, unable to look Adam directly in the eye.

"Don't thank me."

"But you made me realize she wasn't looking out for me." I step closer.

He turns his body so we're not facing one another. "I guess I still like to piss your mom off."

So what just happened used to be a normal occurrence? I nod, not remembering any of their previous spats.

"Plus, I can't find closure if you don't remember why you walked out on me."

"I wish I had answers for you," I say, still amazed that I walked out on him. Why would I ever leave him when everything inside me says I love him, that we were happy? "Do you have photos? Of us that I could have?"

His gaze rises and he sighs but nods.

"Could I see them?"

"Sure. I can bring them here for you."

I shuffle my feet, unable to believe how uncomfortable and awkward it is between us. All I want to do is jump into his arms and hold him tight. "Where did we live?"

He's silent for so long, I'm unsure if he's going to respond. "I rent it out on one of those home-sharing websites. I can't take you there."

"Oh, I hoped it might help. Maybe I could drive by the outside?"

"Ask one of my siblings. They can..." He inhales deeply and squeezes his eyes closed. "I'll take you there Saturday. I'm off and I can get you in before the next renter comes."

"That would be great," I say, unsure what else to say. "Thank you."

"Stop thanking me." His phone rings and he pulls it out of his pocket, looking at the screen. "I might want your memory to come back more than you. I gotta go." His thumb slides over the screen as he walks away. "Hey, baby," he answers and climbs into his truck.

I act distracted and not fazed at all that he uses some generic term of endearment for the new girl in his life as a memory resurfaces. He was more original at the age of sixteen.

Chapter Seven

Lucy

Junior Year of High School

"What are you guys going as?" Cora asked when we placed our lunch trays on the table and sat down.

I eyed Adam, who was in deep conversation with Toby about the homecoming game. He didn't much care about the dance, but more about beating our rivals, Lake Starlight High School.

"I was searching all the Broadway shows last night." Cora cracked open her pop and took a sip.

"And what did you decide?"

She shrugged. "I'd like to do *Best Little Whorehouse in Texas*, but an expulsion isn't going to help me get out of this town."

Cora had wanted to get the hell out of Sunrise Bay and Alaska for as long as I'd known her. Her grades were good, plus she was the student body president and played on the girls' soccer team. It was bound to happen for her. But her future saddened me because I never wanted to leave Sunrise Bay. I loved our town and everyone who lived there.

"Then there's *Kinky Boots*." She laughed, and I loved hearing her laugh because it had a magical way of making everyone around her happy. It was one of the reasons she was the class president.

"You could get away with *Chicago* probably." I ate my fry and side-glanced at Adam as he pulled a notebook out of his backpack and wrote down a football play for Toby and a few of the other players crowded around them.

"That's a good idea. At least I won't be in some big puffy dress," Cora said, then elbowed me. "What's Adam think?"

"He doesn't even care about the dance. I was asking him last night about what we could go as and all he could talk about was how much they had to win and how Nick isn't fast enough off the line—"

"Give him a break. He's under a lot of pressure. I mean, his brother got a scholarship to a huge school last year."

Cora was right. Xavier, Adam's brother, had gotten a full ride to the University of Michigan the year before. Everyone in town sent him off with a parade and the expectation that he'd be returning as a professional player. Adam had gotten Xavier's spot as starting varsity quarterback and he'd only been a junior. But he felt the pressure to continue the winning streak his brother had started three years ago.

"I just wish there was a balance," I said, watching Adam with his friends and the way his teammates hung on every word, as if he was Xavier.

Cora elbowed me again. Being my best friend meant she knew when to pull me back to sanity and tell me to stop obsessing. "Tell me. What do you want to be?"

I sat up straighter, excited to tell her my idea. Only Cora would understand why I chose who I did.

"Frenchy," I whispered so no one would take my idea.

Cora stared blankly.

"From *Grease*," I clarified.

She nodded and a smile formed on her face. I knew she'd get it. "Is this just your brilliant idea to get your hair dyed pink?"

I nodded.

"Susan won't let you."

"It's for a character, and as she says, anything worth doing is worth doing the best." I smiled proudly as I bit into my fry.

"She's going to lock you in your room," Cora said.

She had a point. My mom was controlling and I'd been trying to convince her for the last month to let me dye my hair pink. She always said absolutely not.

"Hey." Adam kissed my cheek and threw his backpack on the table. "What am I missing?" He stole a fry and popped it into his mouth.

His sweet eyes and boyish grin stirred butterflies in my stomach even though we'd been a couple for almost a year.

"That you're about to be Doody." Cora laughed.

"Doody?" Adam asked.

Toby threw his backpack on the table and leaned across the table. "Who are you gonna be, Shefield?" he asked Cora.

"What do you care?" she snipped.

Those two hated one another.

"Rumor is you're going with Justin?"

She smiled and nodded. Justin was class vice president, and although he was a great guy, he wasn't right for Cora. Cora bossed him around and he followed her around like being vice president meant kissing the president's ass. "I am. And I heard you're taking Amara?"

"Yep." He stole a fry from her plate, and she narrowed her eyes.

"Adam, you really need to improve your social circle." Cora slid her tray away, but we all knew that Toby would try to snag another just to piss her off before he left.

"What are we gonna be?" Adam asked me, straddling the bench so he was as close to me as he could be without getting in trouble. His hand absentmindedly ran along my lower back.

"I already told you, you're Doody," Cora said, laughing again.

"What is she talking about, Luce?" Adam took a chicken nugget from my plate and swallowed it in one bite.

"Well, I figured we could go as characters from *Grease*." I shrugged.

"Isn't that a movie? I thought the theme was Broadway?" Toby asked.

"And to think people say you're a dumb jock." Cora rolled her eyes. "It was a Broadway play first."

"Thank you for the useless tidbit of information." Toby narrowed his eyes.

"Well, you should expand your knowledge to other things besides a pigskin ball that flies through the air."

Adam snaked his hand around my waist and tugged me closer. I loved that he wasn't embarrassed to show people how much he loved me. Everyone in town thought we were young and blinded by hormones, but what I felt for Adam wasn't puppy love.

"What is she talking about?" he whispered and sneaked in another kiss right below my ear.

"If you don't stop, we're going to get detention for being handsy."

He laughed. "They're not going to chance the game."

Sadly, he wasn't wrong. "I want to be Frenchy."

"Frenchy?"

"You're going to drop out and go to beauty school?" Toby asked.

"Whoa, look whose light bulb just turned on!" Cora gave him a saccharine smile.

"Tell me, Shefield, what's a bootleg play?"

"Right after you tell me the chemical formula for glucose?"

"Forget them, who is Frenchy?" Adam asked.

I slid my tray over to him because he would eat the majority of my lunch anyway. "She's a character from *Grease*."

"I thought Sandy was from *Grease*?"

I was surprised that he'd been paying attention when I made him watch the movie with Chevelle and me a few months earlier. I'd thought he was just trying to feel me up under the blanket the whole time. I guess he could multi-task. "She's the main character."

He ate the rest of my chicken nuggets as though he hadn't devoured his entire lunch minutes earlier.

"Frenchy is the one who dyes..." I nodded and he shook his head. "Luce, we're Danny and Sandy, not Frenchy and whoever."

"Doody, and Doody is still a T-bird."

"But he's not *the* T-bird. Plus, if you're Sandy, you can wear black leather pants." His eyebrows waggled up and down.

I rolled my eyes. "But then I can't dye my hair."

Adam understood how badly I'd wanted to dye my hair

since a few other girls in our school had done it. But it meant I had to bleach the color out of my hair first, so my mom was against it.

"I'll admit I like that it will piss your mom off," he said, which I understood.

Mom hated that I was dating Adam and tried to convince me daily how we were just young love and nothing would come of it. But I knew different.

"So can we?" I asked.

He blew out a breath and glanced at Toby across the table, who had somehow gotten his hands on Cora's tray.

"You might as well put a 'kick me' sign on your back," Toby remarked.

I put my palm in the air to shut him up. Adam glanced from Toby to me. I bit my lip and gave him my best "come on" look.

He sighed. "Fine."

I threw my arms around his neck and cast kisses all along his face. "Thank you. Thank you. Thank you."

"You owe me," he whispered.

"Miss Davis. Mr. Greene. Please separate." Mr. Turner stood at the end of our table.

We moved apart and apologized.

The lunch bell went off and Adam picked up my tray as Toby took Cora's. I had science with Toby and Adam had math.

Adam glanced both ways down the hall at our lockers. "See you later, French."

He kissed me right on the lips, then slid his tongue inside my mouth. Afterward, he winked and took off down the hall, swallowed up by the class who loved their star football player.

I held my books to my chest and sighed. He was mine.

"You really have him by the balls," Toby said next to me.

I pushed off the locker and walked with him to science. "It's called love. You should find it."

He cackled so loudly, everyone looked at us. "You live in some imaginary bubble. Both of you."

Toby was just one of many in our town who didn't believe in us, but I was sure we'd prove them wrong. We weren't typical high school sweethearts and they'd all see it at our ten-year reunion when Adam and I had a houseful of kids and were still as in love as we were that day.

I guess maybe I was the one who'd been wrong.

Chapter Eight

Adam

"Hey, baby," I answer my phone, walking away from Lucy.

"Why are you calling me baby?" my stepsister Nikki asks.

I climb into my truck and put the keys in the ignition, trying not to look up, but I fail like always, taking one last glimpse of Lucy as she stands in the middle of the parking lot in her mud-covered clothes, staring at her feet.

"What's up?" I ask.

"Don't play stupid. Did you think I was Alicia or something?"

"Nope."

My stepsister won't ever find out that I called her baby to somehow get back at Lucy. What for? For the part of her that doesn't remember that she broke my heart, I guess. I'm a terrible human being.

"Whatever," she says. "Anyway, I'm calling to warn you

that I'm outing this whole Lucy situation tomorrow morning on my show."

I blow out a breath and pull out of the parking lot, putting her on Bluetooth once I know Lucy can't hear our conversation outside of the car. "Of course you are."

"I can't let people say I'm playing favorites. Cade already got those rumblings started when I held the story on Presley last year."

I roll my eyes. Nikki is a radio personality at the local station, and part of her schtick is this gossip piece she calls the "Scandals of Sunrise."

"It's fine. What are you going to say?"

I can't blame Nikki. Cade despises what she does, but someone in this town is gonna spread the gossip. As far as I'm concerned, it might as well be a family member. Plus, it's better than one gossipy secret turning into a game of telephone and becoming something else entirely at the other end. At least with Nikki's show, everyone knows she tries to make sure her sources are legit.

"I'm just saying that she's back and doesn't remember why she left. It might help her too. Everyone in town expects her to be her old self and open her arms and hearts to everyone. I heard some stirrings at The Grind this morning about how she's turned cold and mean. Then someone from the Gossip Brigade told that person that she doesn't know who she is."

Fuck. Figures everything would get convoluted. I'm actually thankful Nikki will get the real story out there. "Well, thanks for the warning."

"Sure thing. Figured you two would want to know, so if you see her, maybe you can tell her."

My hands tighten on the steering wheel. "I'm not gonna see her."

"I heard she was going back to Idaho?" She's digging for information now. "And just so you know, Ethel and Dori had her cornered at Two Brothers and an Egg this morning, so watch out. You know those two."

I huff, wondering if Grandma could work her magic with her friend Dori. But unless I fall off a horse too and forget the pain Lucy caused me, there's no hope of rekindling a relationship between us. I'd always be afraid she'd up and leave me again when she regained her memories.

"You'd have to ask her. I'm cool with it, Nikki, but I'm not gonna be one of your sources."

"I was just being a nice sister. It's a fine line." There's an edge to her tone, which I understand.

"You do know one day you're going to find yourself on the other side of this, right? And then you'll feel how we do." I stop at a stop sign and turn right.

"It's not like I'm someone famous and I'm telling the whole world, Adam. It's Sunrise Bay."

Having this argument with her is ridiculous, especially since I don't really care. I'm just not gonna let her swindle information out of me. "I gotta go to work."

"Fine."

I hang up without saying goodbye like any good sibling in a snit with another one.

I don't really have to go to work today, so I go to the only place where someone might be on my side. To people who understand what it was like to be left behind with no explanation.

After driving through town to the other side of the bay, I pull in front of the house to find her outside with chalk in her hand, drawing on the driveway. I park the truck at the bottom of the driveway and climb out.

"I figured I'd see you soon," Cora says, dropping the chalk and standing.

"Yeah, what the fuck is going on, right?" I glance at the little guy at her ankles. "Sorry."

She shakes her head and steps around her son, hugging me. "It's okay. His dad has a worse mouth than that." She squeezes me tightly then releases me.

I sit down on the stairs to the porch. "Tell me what to do."

She sighs and sits next to me. "I'm not sure."

Cora tells me how she ran into Lucy downtown earlier with my grandma and Dori. That she remembered Cora doesn't surprise me—the two were best friends. But Lucy didn't remember Cora being married or being pregnant with Brody.

Hard to believe Brody is already almost a year old. He's like the marker of when my life went to shit and my best friend started a new segment of his.

I rise from the stairs and sit with Brody on the cold ground. Taking a piece of chalk, I draw a little something. I haven't drawn in forever.

"He tries to eat the chalk sometimes, but you know me. I'm still gonna be the crazy mom who tries to get him to read by age two."

I laugh because that's Cora. I was as surprised as Toby when she decided to stay home with Brody after he was born. Cora was always determined to conquer the world. The classmate most likely to succeed outside of Sunrise Bay. She went away to college but returned after a couple years. Ended up having a few classes with Toby and somehow their dislike for each other turned into love.

"Nothing wrong with that," I say, drawing a sun and clouds, a mountain range in the back.

"You were always good at drawing," Cora says, sitting down and plopping Brody in her lap. She takes the chalk out of his mouth and places it in the bin closest to me.

"A long time ago."

"Not that long ago. You're only twenty-five."

Lucky for me, Toby pulls up in the driveway.

"It's nice that real estate lets him swing by anytime," I say.

She laughs. "I think Brody and I cramp his style. Before the baby, I think he enjoyed coming home when I was still at work. Now he just comes home for lunch every day."

"Greene, what the hell are you doing at my house in the middle of the day?" Toby walks around his fancy SUV in a suit.

Sometimes I wonder if it was Cora who got his act together, but happiness looks good on them both. "Just chalking it up with my guy, Brody."

"She was trying to get a crayon in his hand the other day." He bends down and kisses the top of Cora's head before bending farther to pluck Brody out of his mom's lap and throw him up in the air.

"Careful, he just ate chalk," Cora says.

"Just let the kid enjoy life." Toby holds Brody above his head, then brings him down. I'd hoped Brody would've done me a solid and thrown up on his dad just to bring some humor to my life, but all he's got is a drooling chin.

Cora stands, brushing her butt off with her hands. "I'll go fix lunch. You staying, Adam?"

"Yeah, he is," Toby answers for me.

"I guess I am."

Cora takes Brody and disappears inside, and Toby sits on the stairs.

"So?" Toby asks.

"She's back." I throw my head in my hands, tugging at the strands of my hair. "I have no idea how to handle all this. She thinks we're still married. She thinks we're happy."

Toby sighs, resting his forearms on his thighs, leaning his body forward like me. "Maybe this is some cosmic force bringing you guys back together. Karma or some shit like that."

I tip my head up to look at him, giving him a 'what the hell are you talking about?' expression.

"I'm serious, you and Lucy, you guys were just so... perfect together."

I stand. "Until she left."

"I still think there's a reason for that, and she's just not saying what it is."

Toby and his damn theories. I think he doesn't want to see the situation for what it is because of fear. Fear that if Lucy could up and leave me one day, then Cora could do the same.

"She stopped loving me. I didn't make her happy. And losing her memories doesn't change that."

He leans back, his forearms on the step above where he's sitting. "I'm not suggesting it does, but let's say she never regains that memory? You could get what you've wanted all this time."

"What?" My head whips in his direction.

"It's not like you're a vault. I know you still love her."

"I've moved on. I've got Alicia now."

He chuckles. "You don't love Alicia."

"I could... maybe."

"Bullshit. I hate to give you the bad news, but there's been one woman your entire life, and that's Lucy Davis."

I refrain from saying she's technically still a Greene. That would just make his point further.

"Maybe if you admit that to yourself, you could think more clearly."

"And what would you do, oh wise one?" I cross my arms.

"If it was Cora, you mean?"

I blow out an annoyed breath. "Yes, if it was Cora."

"Easy. I'd go along with the story that we're still married, and we'd live happily ever after. Then if she ever did get her memory back, I'd just have to lock her in a closet until she came to her senses."

"You'd deceive her?" A smile tips my lips because I actually envision it happening.

"She's my world. Hell, if it wasn't for her, I'd be facedown in my own vomit. That woman saw something in me I didn't even know was there."

"I'm not sure any of us knew it was there."

He picks up a piece of chalk on the stair and throws it at me. "Hey, asshole, you're the one who wants advice."

"Not if it includes ignoring reality."

The door opens and Cora comes out, then she hands us each a bottle of water.

"Where's the beer?" I ask.

"It's noon." She sits down next to her husband and he swings his arm between her legs, resting the side of his body against hers and his hand against her calf. "You two fix this?" Doubt is clear in her voice.

"Don't lose your memory, otherwise Toby is gonna lock you up in a closet. He can't live without you."

She looks at him and kisses him. "Same."

"You're both delusional." I shake my head and they laugh.

Cora stands from the stairs and meets me at the bottom. "I hate to be the bearer of bad news, but I am the smartest one here, so here it goes. You ready to hear it?"

"I'm ready for anything," I say.

"You need to help her. I know that you might end up right where you were a year ago at the end of this, but you know as much as we do that you're going to help her. You love her still, so let's stop pretending that you hate her and wish her ill. It's killing you to see her struggling."

Goddamn, Cora. "I fucking hate you."

Toby laughs. "See why I'd lock her in a closet?"

I shake my head as Cora places her hand on my shoulder. "We all know how much you hate the unexpected, and where this will end up, I don't think anyone can predict. She could regain the memory of why she left and decide that it was the right thing to do. Or she might never regain the memory of why she left you. You might just fall in love with her all over again. She might be a completely different Lucy than we know. But stop the act and get it going, because the longer you try to act like you don't care, the longer until it's over."

It's not that Cora doesn't have a point. She should've continued her schooling to get her doctorate in psychology.

"What do you expect me to do?" I ask.

"She remembers you, she remembers me, and although she might not want to, she'll probably remember Toby." She gives me a wink.

"I'm a memorable guy," he says.

"It's a great start. Maybe you take her to the cabin. Walk her to where you got married. Show her memories of her life here with you."

My jaw clenches when I think about how I'll be inflicting pain on myself if I do that.

"She shouldn't be at the inn. She should be sleeping at the house. She should be surrounded with memories of the two of you."

"Fuck, Cora." I push my hand through my hair.

Her shoulders rise in a cocky shrug. "Just say I'm right."

"Am I really going to do this?" I say more to myself than her.

"I promise you this. If this ends badly, I'll gladly serve you a beer at noon next time." She smiles wide and slaps me on the back.

I look at Toby, and he's looking at her as though she hung his fucking moon. Damn them and their happiness. Their perfect family.

She won't have to serve me a beer because if this goes bad, I'll be bent over my brothers' bar with an empty bottle of whiskey in my hand.

Chapter Nine

Lucy

"Two months, Luce. That's all you're getting. And I want you to know I do not agree with this decision." Mom stands outside her Uber in the parking lot of the SunBay Inn, her bags already in the trunk. "Mandi wouldn't take my card to pay for you, so clean up after yourself. Don't make them cater to you."

"I won't."

She nods a few times, still looking put out. I can't let her get on a plane and go back to Idaho with us like this.

"Mom," I say, stopping her before she climbs into the back seat. "I'm not trying to upset you."

She sighs. "I wanted to spare you from this, but I see now I can't. It's your life. You made that clear to me a long time ago."

I rush into her arms and squeeze her tightly, hoping the friction that was there before I left Adam will evaporate this time around. I want a different outcome if I decide Sunrise Bay is where I want to be.

"I love you," I say, meaning every word.

"Just be careful, sweetie." She runs her hand down my back and releases me sooner than I would have.

I step back and she slides into the car, waving one last time before the Uber pulls out of the parking lot.

My phone dings with a reminder. I forgot that my neurologist wanted to get on a video call to talk to me now that I've been here a few days. I'm still caked in dry mud and there's no time for a shower.

I head into the inn, thankful I'm staying in town. Climbing the stairs, I go into my room and see that my mom made her bed before she left. I grab my computer and sit on my bed, positioning it on top of a pillow.

After I dial Dr. Lipstein, his bald head pops up on the screen.

"Lucy," he says, positioning his computer straighter.

"Hi, Dr. Lipstein," I say.

"How is Alaska?" He leans back in his chair.

One thing I love about Dr. Lipstein is the fact that he's laid back. He never makes me feel as though there's something wrong with me. From day one, he's made it clear that hopefully my memories will come back, but they may not and that's okay too. My first appointment after I was discharged from the hospital was with a support group he suggested where some people have regained all their memories and others who haven't regained any. Seeing those people thriving made me think I could too. But it also spurred me to want to come here to Alaska.

"It's okay." I shrug.

"Just okay?"

"My mom left to go back to Idaho and I'm going to stay here."

A small smile creases his lips.

"What?"

He chuckles. "I had a feeling things wouldn't go how you predicted up there."

"What does that mean?"

His head tips right and left as though he's unsure how to say whatever it is he wants to say. "I've been doing this job a long time. Something about your mom's position on you returning there just flagged me. That's all. When someone loses their memory, unfortunately, it can some-times bring people back into their life in a way they weren't a part of it before. You'd returned to your family after you left Sunrise Bay, but I think there's a lot to uncover while you're there. A large part of who you used to be."

"I'm married," I blurt.

His eyes widen. "Your parents didn't tell you?"

I nod, still annoyed that my mom tried to erase this part of my life. "I guess I left him about a year ago. I don't remember why, and I really want to."

"Did he approach you when you got to town or did someone tell you?"

I shake my head with a proud smile.

"You remembered?"

"It was crazy. My mom and I were walking through town and there were all these people because it's the day before tourist season starts and the entire town comes out. And I turned my head to the right and saw Adam. I couldn't get to him fast enough."

"And how did Adam react?"

My smile dims. "Confused. When I saw him, I felt like I was still married. I forgot for a moment that more than a year had passed since I'd even been in Sunrise Bay."

"I see the disappointment on your face, and you should

know that's to be expected. You remembered him and that you were married. Anything else?"

"Ever since, little things from my past involving him have come back. A memory from when we were thirteen, and another one at sixteen."

"Lucy, that's amazing. I assume that's why you're staying in Sunrise Bay?"

I nod, biting my lip. "I think this is where I need to be for now."

"I agree. I'm sorry your mother did not though."

I shrug, appeased that Dr. Lipstein agrees I should stay. "From what I gather, she never came to my wedding. She doesn't like my husband or his family."

He nods.

"I'm mad because she was trying to keep me from remembering."

He nods again.

"I mean, how could she take that away from me?" Tears slip down my cheeks. I'm unsure who I can talk to about this. The fact I have to resort to talking to my neurologist says how desperate I am for a friend. I thought my mom was on my side, marching along to get me back to who I was, and now I've found out she was trying to steer me away from the very place that would help me.

"Lucy, it's hard to understand. Sometimes family members think they're helping you. I'm sure she was trying to spare you the pain of reliving the part of your life when you left your husband. I don't think she was being malicious."

"Are you saying you agree with what she did?" I swipe my tears away with the backs of my hands.

He shakes his head. "No, but I do understand. I think everyone has things in their life they'd like to forget. Maybe it has more to do with her than you." He shrugs. "But let's focus on the now. You're there. Somewhere safe, I hope?"

"I'm at an inn."

"Good. I'm sure you had friends there. Have you reconnected?"

I nod. "Yes." Maybe Cora? I mean, Mandi was always nice, but she's Adam's sister.

"You need people you can trust."

I still trust Adam, although he hates me for leaving him. Not that I blame him. I'd hate me too.

"Yeah, I know."

"Then just enjoy your time while you're there. Don't pressure yourself. Surround yourself with people and things that are familiar to you, and maybe some things will come back. But like I told you, you might never get every memory back. You may never remember what happened with you and your husband."

My shoulders slump. That's the one thing I really want to know.

A soft knock on the door interrupts us.

"Okay, let's meet at the same time next week unless you need me. Does that sound good?"

"Sounds good."

"Keep fighting, Lucy. You're doing amazing." He winks, and we both say goodbye.

Another knock sounds on the door and I rush off the bed to answer.

I swing the door open and step back, surprised. "Adam?"

ADAM WALKS in and his scent floats by me as he passes. I close my eyes and inhale, a feeling of safety falls over me.

Maybe I shouldn't trust that feeling though, like Dr. Lipstein said.

He sits on the edge of my mom's bed. "I heard you ran into Cora."

I nod, stepping around him to sit on my bed. I'm sure he doesn't want me on the same bed as him, although it's where my body yearns to go.

"She has a baby," I say as if he doesn't know that.

"Brody. Yeah. He's a cool kid."

"They were going to story time." I hate that talking to him feels awkward. I don't know what to say.

"Do you remember that she's married to Toby?" He glances at me, his forearms resting on his thighs and his fingers weaved together.

"She told me."

"So you don't remember their wedding?"

I shake my head.

"They got married after us. What's your last memory?" he asks.

I sit up straighter on the bed, crossing my legs. "Little things have been coming back. I remember your thirteenth birthday party, and homecoming when we went as Frenchy and Doody. I don't remember our wedding, but I know you're my husband. Is that weird? It is."

He shrugs. "I'm not a doctor."

"I just talked to him about my mom and what she was doing. I should apologize."

"For her? Please. You don't have to apologize for your mom. At least not to me."

I nod, unsure what he wants, why he's here.

He rises from the bed and paces. "I'm going to help you, but I want to make a few things clear."

"Help me?" My forehead wrinkles.

He stops and stares at me. "When you left, I moved into the house with my brothers and started renting out our place, but I made arrangements for the renters who were coming Saturday to stay somewhere else and I've canceled the rest of the renters for the season. That way you can move in."

"Move into our home?" I've been dying to go there, but I never thought he'd allow me to stay there.

"It's where our life was. And I can take you to the places that were important to you."

"You know them?"

His face scrunches up and he rolls his eyes. "You were my wife. You were my fucking world since I was thirteen. Yeah, I know them."

"Oh... okay."

"But I have a girlfriend now, so I want to make it clear nothing is gonna happen between us." He pulls some papers out of his back pocket and tosses them on the bed. "We're not a couple. And you need to sign these."

I pick up what I see now are divorce papers and sob inside. Our names written on the left-hand side with vs. between them. I never thought I'd see anything but an ampersand between our names. This makes it look like we're enemies and I've always seen us as a united front.

I toss them on the other bed. "I don't want these."

"It's not really your choice." He runs a hand through his dark hair.

A flash of a memory of us on a couch, his head in my lap, flashes through my mind. My fingers mindlessly ran through his hair while he told me a story about a bear. I laughed and his arm stretched up and pulled my head down for a kiss.

I shake my head. "I'm not signing them. Not until I know why."

"Why what?" He throws his hands in the air.

"Why I left. It doesn't feel like something I would've done."

His fists clench. "Ask anyone in this town. You did."

"Well, I don't remember, so I'm not signing them until I find out why."

He stares at me with flames igniting his hazel eyes. "Jesus, Luce...y, I'm trying to fucking help you here. Give me a little something in return."

I stand. "I'm not giving up on us."

"You already did. A year ago." He steps forward.

"That was then." I stomp my foot.

We end up chest to chest, and he says, "Meet me half-way. Let me salvage a little bit of my self-respect."

I lay my hand on his chest. His heartbeat pounds against my palm and he swallows, clenching his jaw. But he doesn't fling my hand off of him. That has to be a good sign. I can feel that there's still an underlying current that's alive between us. "Do you love me, Adam?"

He never looks away. "Sign the papers, Lucy."

"I'll make you a deal." I run my hand down his chest.

His hand wraps around my wrist, stopping me from going farther, but still he doesn't remove it from him. "No deal. Sign."

"My mom gave me two months here. I'll sign them then. No matter what happens. Whether I remember or don't. In two months, if you still want a divorce, I'll sign."

Our eyes are locked, and I sigh, seeing him actually soaking me in. All the other times I've been around him, I felt as though he was actively trying to ignore my presence, but here I am, right in front of him, and it feels as though he's *really* seeing me for the first time since I came back.

I inch up on my toes and he releases my wrist, his hand falling to my hip. My breath is shallow as we slowly, so slowly, move closer. When our mouths are inches apart, he releases me, stepping back and storming over to the door.

"I'll pick you up at nine on Saturday." He slams the door behind him.

I pick up the divorce papers and toss them in the trash. I'll never sign them.

Chapter Ten

Adam

I'm on my way to meet Alicia for breakfast the next morning when Nikki's segment "Scandals of Sunrise" comes on the radio. I'm tempted to change the station, but I want to hear firsthand what she tells the town.

"Hey, Sunrise Bayers, it's your host, Nikki Greene, with my co-host, Chip. Say hi, Chip."

"Hi," he says in that grumpy tone I think all the listeners love.

"How was your night?"

"Fine."

"What did you do?"

"Nothing."

"Come on, Chip. You had to have done something. Watch television or anything?"

"Nope."

"You're telling me you didn't even check out *The Bachelorette* last night? I thought that was your fave." She laughs. Chip doesn't. But she's used to it—these are the roles they've perfected. "Well, I have some news for everyone that I need to share."

"Do tell," Chip says as if he's thumbing through a newspaper and barely paying attention to her.

"Lucy Greene, aka Lucy Davis, is back in town. I know. I know. Most of you already saw her a few nights ago. As you all know, I'm Adam's stepsister, so I was nice enough to let the excitement from her arrival die down so I could figure out what's really going on before I reported on it. Exactly why did she greet Adam like nothing had happened when in fact she left him, causing him to spiral down into despair?"

"His new girl is a looker," Chip says.

I chuckle for the first time. Alicia is hot, can't argue that. *But she's not Lucy.*

I curse my subconscious and go back to listening.

"Alicia is pretty. But rumor has it that Lucy lost her memory after an accident and she's here in Sunrise Bay to try to recover it. It's no secret that Lucy's family and my family don't see eye to eye."

"She hates your family's guts," Chip chimes in.

"Yes, but the wicked witch has left Oz after a fight outside SunBay Inn."

"Tell Mandi that the fish fry on Friday was excellent."

"Chip, let's stay on task." Nikki pauses. "But yeah, I agree about the fish fry."

"Told you so."

"Anyway, back to Sunrise Bay's own Cory and Topanga. I love my stepbrother, but he's been cold to Lucy the last few days."

"A broken heart is hard to overcome."

I shake my head at the fact he's actually contributing to this.

"True. But I heard a juicy piece of information last night."

"Just spit it out," Chip says.

"Adam was seen going up to Lucy's room at the inn after her mom left. And that's all I'm going to say about that."

My hands tighten on the steering wheel.

"You're purposely stirring up gossip."

"It's called 'Scandals of Sunrise,' Chip. Anyway, listeners out there, if you catch sight of Lucy, maybe tell her a story to help her remember how loved she was in Sunrise Bay. After all, Adam might not realize it now, but he'd love it if she stuck around. That's it for me. Chip, what's the fishing weather gonna be like the next few days?"

Annoyed, I park my truck, grab my phone, and walk into the square. Two Brothers and an Egg is packed, but Alicia texted that she already had a table in the back. All eyes follow me as I make my way into the restaurant. Tad, one of the owners, pats me on the back on the way back to the table.

"You had the station on?" I ask.

"Sorry you're the topic, but we always listen in the morning. Go have a seat next to your looker." He laughs.

I ignore the stares from a table full of moms who are my parents' age. *Thanks a lot, Nikki.*

I sit down across from Alicia, but her head is buried in her phone as though she doesn't know I've arrived.

"Hey," I say.

"Oh. Hey." She tucks her phone into her purse.

"You heard?"

She nods, wetness pooling in her eyes. Hell. I came here to end this between us amicably. Or at the very least put us on hold until I get things settled with Lucy.

"How is she?" she asks.

I open my mouth, but thankfully Tad arrives with his pad of paper and pen poised. I'm starving.

I nod for Alicia to go first and she says, "Just a muffin."

"Brad did something magical in there this morning," Tad says.

"What exactly are you talking about?" I ask him.

"Get your mind out of the gutter. It's a streusel, cinnamon concoction you're going to love." He winks at Alicia.

"Great." She smiles.

"I'll have—"

He jots down an order for me without me saying anything. "I've got it."

"But I want—"

He points at the sign that says no arguing with the manager. I shake my head and he leaves.

"He's funny," Alicia says.

I met her in Anchorage at some speed dating thing I did once I finally realized I had to get back out there but didn't want it up for public consumption in this town. I purposely only dated her in Anchorage and thankfully we never ran into anyone. Once I knew maybe there was something between us, we had some dates here in Sunrise Bay, but it hasn't been that long. And I'm thinking I should've waited longer because she shouldn't have to endure what she is right now.

"He and his brother are twins. Tad and Brad. They've lived here their entire lives. Own this place." I lean forward and lower my voice. "I'm sorry about my sister's report. I'm going to tell you everything."

She holds up her hand to stop me before I can say anything else. "Can I ask you a question?"

I lean back in my chair. "Sure."

"Do you still love her? And I don't mean like you care for her. I'm sure when you've been with someone as long as you were, you're probably going to care on some level."

Has she been checking up on Lucy and me? Because I never told Alicia anything about us or how long we'd been together.

She must see something in my face because she sighs. "It isn't hard to find information on Adam Greene and Lucy Davis from Sunrise Bay with the Internet. Your wedding announcement is online and pretty much gave me all the information I needed."

I nod.

"So?"

I busy myself taking my silverware out of my napkin and placing the napkin on my lap. "I do love Lucy, I can't deny that. When she left me, I was ruined. But where we stand now? I don't know."

"And that leaves me at the curb," she says, her gaze moving out the front window.

"I'm not gonna lie, I came here to be straight with you. I like you, Alicia, but the only reason I was in her room at the inn was to tell her that I would help her regain her memories as best I can."

"Great." She exhales a big breath and falls back into her chair.

"I don't expect you to understand or care for that part."

"Breakfast is served!" Tad interrupts, putting a muffin with a side of fruit in front of Alicia. She doesn't seem to notice that he gave her something extra. Tad and his damn soft heart. He sets down pancakes, an omelet, and hash browns in front of me. "Enjoy, you two."

"I don't understand why just because she lost her

memory, it's your problem. I mean, she left you, Adam, not the other way around. You owe her nothing."

The venom in her voice takes me by surprise. Up until this moment, she's always been sweet, but then again, we've only been dating a little while. Although I guess if she had an ex-husband I'd never heard about show up and act like they were still married, I'd be confused and hurt too. But it's not as though I thought I'd ever see Lucy again.

So I say as gently as I can, "I'm not just doing it for her. I'm doing it for myself too. I have to find out why she left me."

She never touches her muffin or her fruit, crossing her arms. "Why?"

I'm growing annoyed by her response. We were never serious. I mean, we never discussed being exclusive or even did anything physical together besides kissing.

"Because I just do." My answer is weak, but it should be enough to get her off my back.

"Ridiculous. You understand all she's going to do is use you to regain her memory, then the reason she left you will come out and you'll be kicked to the curb—again."

Her comments sting and I lash out before I can think better of it. "Well if you're still there, we can start over."

"Nice." She narrows her eyes.

"I'm sorry. I shouldn't have said that. Let me clear it up." I set down my fork and knife. "I understand what I'm chancing here. I've thought about it. I have no idea what's at the end of this road, but if I don't follow it, I'll always regret it."

She shakes her head and puts her napkin on the table. "Well, good luck to you." Rising from the table, she glances around the restaurant before her gaze lands on me.

"I'm sor—"

She bends down and presses her lips to mine, her tongue sliding into my mouth. It takes me by surprise after the conversation we just had, so I'm slow on the uptake. I put my hand on her shoulder to push her away, but she breaks the kiss off first.

"Have a nice life, Adam," she whispers. "And fuck you."

She steps away from the table.

"Want to wrap up that muffin and fruit?" Tad asks, but I don't hear Alicia answer.

I shake my head and pick up my silverware until the door chimes and the diner quiets. I glance over my shoulder and see Lucy walking in. Fuck me, is that why Alicia gave me that goodbye kiss? As revenge?

"Hey, Lucy, remember when I fixed your bike during the Fourth of July parade?" someone asks.

"How about when you sold me Girl Scout cookies? I was always your highest orderer," someone says.

"Lucy, let me get you one of Brad's muffins," Tad offers.

"The first time you fished was on my boat, remember?" someone else asks her.

She's polite to everyone, saying whether she does or does not remember what they're talking about. She's in her running gear again. I wonder when she picked up that habit. The Lucy I knew hated running.

"Hey, Adam," she says, standing beside my table.

"Hi." I wipe my mouth.

"I hope I'm not the reason Alicia left," she says.

"No, she's got a busy life."

Her gaze falls to the untouched muffin and fruit. "I guess so, since she didn't even eat."

Who am I kidding? Why am I putting on a charade that I'm still with Alicia? "Yeah."

"Well, I was stopping in and I didn't want to not say

hello. I wondered about your work schedule? I know we have to wait for Saturday to get into the cabin, but I thought maybe you could take me to where I used to work or something. Or just tell me a place where I loved to go?"

I close my eyes and groan.

"Sorry, never mind. I'll just figure something else out."

"You used to love the path around the bay. Not to run, but just to clear your head."

She smiles and damn if pleasing her doesn't still make me feel like fucking Superman. I hate that that's still alive inside me. "Thank you."

"Take this with you." Tad hands her a bag with a muffin in it. "On the house."

"Oh no. I couldn't."

"Don't tell me you've forgotten the number one rule here." He points at the sign about no arguing with the manager.

I roll my eyes.

"I haven't. Thanks, Tad." She rises to her tiptoes and kisses his bearded cheek.

He winks and leaves to greet his other customers.

"I should go. Thank you, Adam. I'll see you Saturday."

I nod. "Saturday."

She walks away and I push my plate across the table, not hungry anymore.

"Be careful, you don't eat and that's going to be the next thing on Nikki's radio show." Tad comes by and takes Alicia's plates.

I watch out the window as Lucy gets stopped by the Gossip Brigade on her way to the bay. Maybe it'll take an entire town to bring back her memories. All I know is the faster she remembers, the faster she signs those papers and I can move on with my life.

Chapter Eleven

"You did rip his heart out with your bare hands."
~Jed Greene

Lucy

I'm not twenty-five feet from Two Brothers and an Egg when I'm stopped by the military veterans most people in this town refer to as the Gossip Brigade. You wouldn't think a bunch of old men would spread gossip, but they do any chance they get.

"Lucy, you remember during the Veteran's Day parade how your class handed out little flags?" one of them says.

"Or how about you'd play at the park with my grandson, Owen?"

"I bet you can't forget that time you had me come into your class to talk about the war."

I smile politely. "Thank you all for trying to jog my memory, but I've got somewhere to be. I'll see you guys later." I pat Mr. Wilson's arm and continue my walk toward the bay.

I sigh when I find the path mostly vacant. Almost all the fishing boats are out for the day and the mountains loom over the water on the far side. I walk the path, pulling pieces of my muffin out of the bag and eating them.

The vision of Alicia and Adam kissing is occupying most of the space in my brain. I wanted to walk over there and tug her off him. She saw me through the window. Our eyes locked before she stood and kissed him. Who uses tongue in a breakfast diner during the morning rush?

But I can't stop Adam from having a girlfriend, so all I can do is focus on myself and getting my memory back and hope like hell I'll never have to sign those papers.

Two months seems way too short, especially since it's been three months since my accident and until I got here, nothing much was happening with my recovery.

"Lucy!" the jogger running toward me on the path yells. I recognize her as Amy from the Twisted Stem. She stops running next to me, jogging in place. "Good to see you."

"Same." I smile, not having much context except for knowing who she is.

"Do you remember your wedding flowers? How elaborate you wanted them? I had to have so many flowers shipped in, but it was *so* beautiful. I hope you can remember that because the ceremony was beautiful. Oh, you and Adam..." She stops talking, her eyes widening. "Oh, I'm sorry. I never should have said anything."

"What kind of flowers?"

She smiles. "Pale pink peonies." Her hands go up in the air. "You had them everywhere. Adam said he wasn't going to put one on his lapel because it was so big, but as always, you convinced him." She laughs. "He said it looked like a big pink puffball and you just gave him that look."

I tilt my head. "What look?"

Her smile dims for a second. "The one that got Adam to do whatever you wished."

"Oh." That makes it sound like I forced him to do things he didn't want to do. Did I?

"I didn't mean it like that. Adam likes to do things for you. It makes him happy when you're happy. That's true love." She squeezes my forearm.

No memory of my wedding day comes crashing back, and I'm disappointed.

"I better go," Amy says. "I have another Greene bride coming in this afternoon."

"Oh?"

"Yeah, Cade and Presley. Have you met her yet? You'll love her."

"Briefly. She seemed nice." Although she was looking at me like an alien from outer space. I can only imagine the things Adam and his family might have said to her about me.

"She's the sweetest. And her bookstore." She acts as if she's getting tingles just thinking about it.

I forgot how much the Greenes are looked up to here. How much everyone loves them.

"Good luck. I'm sure they'll love their flowers as much as I did." I pretend I remember, but sadly, I don't. Does that mean something?

"See you around, Lucy. So happy you stayed." She jogs away and I continue down the path.

After fifty feet, I decide to call Dr. Lipstein because I'm annoyed I'm remembering people but not necessarily events. The nurse is nice enough to put me on hold until he's done with a patient, so I walk around the bay a little longer, walking away from groups of people who act as though they want to talk to me.

When Dr. Lipstein comes on the line, he says, "Lucy, did something happen?"

"No, I just had the florist from my wedding stop me and tell me all about the flowers, and although I remember her, I don't remember what the flowers even looked like at my wedding."

He chuckles. "You grew up in Sunrise Bay, Lucy. You might've interacted with that woman many times throughout your life if that town is as small as you say it is. You might not remember her from your wedding, but from another time in your life. Don't force it."

I'm not about to tell Dr. Lipstein about Nikki telling everyone to stop me and tell me a memory as though they'll win a prize if I recall their memory. "So it's okay?"

"Yes. You're making great progress and I believe you're right where you should be, but take it slow. Don't force it. Allow them to come to you when they come to you."

"Okay."

He chuckles again. "I know it can be frustrating."

"Yeah."

"For patients who haven't had the progress you have thus far, we're usually talking about their new future. The one where they need to find out who they are now, not who they were. But I don't want you thinking that way yet. Maybe while you're there, try to discover what you used to love. You never know what can happen. The mind is a tricky place to navigate and there's never one right course of action."

"Thanks, Dr. Lipstein."

"Anytime. Now, go relax. Just because you stayed there doesn't mean your mind will magically recover with the snap of your fingers."

"Okay. Yeah, makes sense."

"Have a great day, Lucy."

"Thanks again."

We hang up, and in my peripheral vision, I catch sight of Fran and her speed walking gang waving me down. I'm glad I remember her right away because I know that I don't want to get cornered by her and her friends. They're always up in everyone's business to the extreme and don't take no for an answer. I head down an exit from the bay to the downtown area. I don't want to be rude, but I just can't right now.

The faster I walk, the louder they call my name.

I refrain from bursting into a sprint. As I step into the square, I spot some tourists strolling around. They're a welcome distraction but not enough to allow me to disappear.

"Hey, Luce…" Jed. Adam's stepbrother. He waves his free hand. The other has a key in it and he's unlocking the brewery. He catches the sight behind me and holds open the door. "We have that appointment, right?"

I glance over my shoulder and sneak inside.

The women reach the door right as I get inside and hide behind one of the long wooden pillars in the middle of the restaurant. I inhale deeply.

"We were trying to get Lucy's attention," Fran says.

"Hey, ladies, maybe her memory is affecting her hearing," Jed says good-naturedly.

One woman laughs.

"Jed Greene!" Fran scolds.

"I'm kidding. You'll have to catch her another time. I have a meeting with her."

"What kind of business do you have with Lucy?" Fran asks.

"You know how we name beers after residents? She's picking her flavor and we're going to name it Minderaser."

They all laugh, and I roll my eyes.

"Now, ladies, you're all looking lovely this morning in your matching tracksuits, but you'll have to excuse me."

I can just see Fran straightening her jacket on her hips as though Jed is checking her out.

"Tell Lucy we have all the stories written down to try to help trigger her," Fran says.

"Oh, I'll tell her, and next time you come in, there's a round on the house."

"Thanks, Jed."

I hear the door shut and lock. Finally I release a breath and come out from behind the post.

"You're thin, but that post doesn't hide you. You know that, right?"

"I guess my eye for dimensions went with my memory and my hearing." I roll my eyes.

He laughs and goes behind the bar. "Glad to see it wasn't your sense of humor that went."

I sit on a barstool and he pulls out two shot glasses, then pours a clear liquid into both.

"Jed, it's, like, nine-thirty," I say.

"I can use it. Cade woke me this morning jabbering about my best man responsibilities. Turns out he's not going to pick between his brothers. So..." He nudges the glass toward me and downs his shot. "Don't tell Adam though."

"Oh, don't worry about that. Our conversations are brief at best." I circle the shot glass in my hands for a moment before downing it, regretting the decision as soon as the burn hits my throat.

"You did rip his heart out with your bare hands."

"Nice."

He pulls a bottle of water from behind the bar and cracks it open before giving it to me. "I'm just speaking the truth. The poor guy was listening to Motown just to forget you."

"Motown?"

He chuckles and props up on the other side of the bar, his foot on a stool behind there. "Yep. The poor bastard was like a billboard ad telling other guys, 'Monogamy sucks, don't do it.'"

"As big as the one out there?" I point to where Cade posted a huge posterboard declaring his love for Presley.

"Wanna make a bet they try to put it up in here? That's happening next to never."

I chuckle and sip my water. "Thank you."

"For what?"

"Saving me from Fran and her gang. Making me laugh. I haven't laughed since I got here. Actually, since the accident maybe."

"Well, losing your memory isn't exactly funny."

"No, but everyone is always so serious with me." I pick at the label on the bottle.

"Do you ever think about what it will be like if you never remember everything?" I stare blankly and he holds up his hands. "Just asking."

I shrug. "It's fine. My doctor is bringing it up to me too. That's more of a probability than me remembering everything."

"So what do you remember?" He looks at me with keen interest.

"Well, I remember people, but not the memories associated with them. Like I know Adam is my husband, but I can't tell you much else. But there have been these moments when I remember things from when we were younger."

He smirks. "You look like you enjoy those memories."

I try to bite down my smile before giving up. "I do. I love him and I'm terrified I'm never going to get him back. What if my memory doesn't return and..." My throat closes up and tears pool in my eyes. "What if I can't tell him why I left him, and he never forgives me, and he just carries on with his life?" A tear slips and I swipe it away with the back of my hand. "I can't bear to live without him. And then there's this girl, Alicia. Do you know her?"

Jed nods, his face showing no emotion.

"How long have they been dating?" I wave it off. "Never mind. You're his brother. I shouldn't be asking you."

"Technically, I'm only his stepbrother," he says, a grin tipping his lips.

I wipe the tears. "I'm sorry. I shouldn't unload all this on you."

"It's okay. It's the most you've ever talked to me."

"Really?"

He nods. "We were friendly and all, but..."

"Then you must really think I'm crazy."

"I think you're confused, and I think you need someone to talk all this out with." He pours another shot. "In my experience, alcohol cures all."

I laugh and he clinks his shot glass with mine, but just as I have the shot glass to my lips, a pounding sound rattles the front door. We both turn toward the noise. Adam is pointing at Jed and swearing.

Jed laughs. "I wouldn't worry about Alicia if I were you." He rounds the bar and unlocks the door.

Adam comes in, takes the shot glass from my lips, and tugs on my hand. "Let's go."

"What? Why? I'm talking with Jed."

Jed leans against the wall by the door with his arms crossed and a smug smile.

"Getting drunk at ten in the morning isn't going to bring back your damn memory," Adam grumbles.

"No, but it was helping her forget the present. Sometimes people need that too," Jed says, waving at me as Adam leads me down the hallway and out the back door.

Chapter Twelve

Adam

"So now you want to talk to me?" Lucy asks when we're standing outside my truck.

Seeing her in the brewery with Jed pissed me off. It could be she doesn't remember that he's my stepbrother or —what am I saying, she probably does, but what if... I can't even allow myself to think about her with anyone else, let alone someone from my family.

"Drinking isn't going to solve this."

Her eyes are rimmed with red and it's clear to me she was crying to Jed. Which makes me angry for a whole other reason. "He suggested it, and last I checked, you just asked me to sign divorce papers."

I roll my eyes, but she holds my gaze. I swear she could scare away a lion.

"Come on. You want to try to remember something, I'm taking you somewhere."

"Where?"

She doesn't get in the truck, so I go around and open the door, waving my hand for her to climb on up. "You'll see."

"How do I know you aren't going to throw me off a cliff?"

"What are you talking about?" I scowl at her.

"Well, you're angry and you want to divorce me. Maybe you've decided to get rid of me. I'm sure I come with some life insurance money."

"You've been with your mom for too damn long. Get in the truck."

She crosses her arms and juts out her hip. I groan. Clearly she didn't lose her stubbornness.

"Please get in the damn truck."

Her eyebrows raise up to her hairline.

"Luce...y!"

"Why do you keep doing that?" Her arms drop to her sides.

"Do what?"

"Put the y after my name. If you used to call me Luce, then just call me that."

I shake my head. "Please just get in the truck."

"Tell me and I will." She walks toward the truck, stopping right in front of me.

She looks so good in her workout gear. The way the leggings hug her ass and show off how strong her thighs are. She used to be able to hold herself up when I'd urge her to wrap them around my waist so I could fuck her against the wall. After we got married, we couldn't keep our hands off one another. Every time I came home, she'd be wearing some lingerie thing or another, and one time she was cooking naked with a see-through plastic apron on. I shift my weight to accommodate for the half chub in my pants now. Great.

"Because I called you that when we were together."

"So now I'm just Lucy to you?"

I nod, unable to tell her that if I allow myself to call her Luce, then I'm admitting to myself that she still has the power to hurt me. It's stupid but necessary.

"Okay," she says and climbs into the truck.

I shut the door behind her and round the back, once again second-guessing agreeing to this stupid plan. Now I have to sit in the cab of my truck and trust myself not to cross the line I desperately want to cross. Especially after my brief stroll down memory lane about how we used to fuck like bunnies in what now feels like another lifetime.

She puts on her seat belt and looks at me with expectancy.

I made a list of places I'd take her, but unfortunately only a few of them are options at this moment. So I bite the bullet and decide to do the one that's the absolute hardest—with the exception of going to the cabin we called home.

"I'm taking you to where I proposed," I say.

"Oh... okay."

She grows silent and the stubborn, sassy side of her disappears while I pull out of the parking lot and drive through downtown Sunrise Bay toward the mountains. God help me.

My stomach feels like a pit of anxiety the entire drive up the mountains. I don't want to relive this moment even if it already haunts me in my head. But maybe this will get me one step closer to the goal of Lucy signing the papers so I can move on with my life.

I park in the lot and glance at her. "Put this on." I reach

back and pull a park ranger sweatshirt from the back seat. "It's colder up here."

She does as I ask and my jaw clenches when I see her in my sweatshirt again.

"Here." I roll up her sleeves while she stares at me through her long dark lashes.

"Thanks."

I swallow past the dryness in my throat and ignore the pull that tells me to kiss her, show her physically how right we are for one another.

"Let's go." I climb out of my truck and grab the backpack I always have with me in case I get stranded anywhere.

She looks around the entrance of the woods. I wait for a flicker of recognition to light her blue irises but see none. She smiles at me. "I'm ready."

"You go first, and I'll follow." I motion for her to walk ahead of me.

She heads up the path, over the broken tree limbs and dead leaves after a long winter. Her fingers brush a few buds on the plants lining the path. "It's already turning green again."

"Summer will be here soon." I try not to look at her too much, but it proves difficult. At least my sweatshirt covers up her amazing ass.

"Are you excited? You always enjoyed summer in the park, right?"

I stop for a moment, but she continues walking, so I start back up.

"I remember you telling me how these kids got themselves in trouble climbing once and you were the big hero who had to save them off the side of a cliff." She looks at me over her shoulder and smiles. "I always found your job so hot."

I refrain from asking her about anything else she might remember. Maybe this is normal—her recalling certain things about me and her feelings.

We hike for another fifteen minutes. Once we get to the last part, she looks at the rock wall that's a little taller than her, then back at me.

"It's a dead end," she says.

I shake my head and step forward, linking my hands and holding them out for her to step up on.

"Oh, this is fun." She jumps to try to see over the ledge, but you can't until you climb up. Using my weaved fingers to push herself up, she ends up bent over with her belly on the ledge, her ass literally in my face.

"I guess some things don't change," I mumble.

"Really? I always look like an octopus trying to put on shoes getting up here?"

I chuckle.

She looks at me over her shoulder. "Let's try again."

"The day I proposed, I bit you on the ass," I admit, more for my own sake than hers.

"I wouldn't have any objections now."

I use both my hands and push her up over the ledge. "Maybe another time."

She tries to hold out her hand to help me up, but I use a tree branch and scale the wall. "I see why you being a park ranger is so hot. That move right there must've gotten you into my pants a lot."

I shake my head, not wanting to think about the two of us together like that, especially with her right here in front of me. But she's right. She always did love any show of physical strength when I was rescuing people or helping her while we hiked.

"It's just past that tree line." I point for her to go in front of me again, wanting this torture to end.

She walks through the trees, looking around as though it's the first time she's been here when in reality we came here tons of times throughout our relationship.

I hear her gasp. "Oh my God."

I've yet to break the perimeter of the trees to see the blue lake surrounded by mountains. I don't have to see it though. I can visualize it. All of it.

"It's so beautiful," she coos.

I walk out of the forest to the view that took my breath away the first time we discovered it. It's still mindboggling that Mother Nature could gift this world such a beautiful sight to discover.

I'd had us climb the wall on a whim that day, not expecting us to find such a special place. I've only been here once over the past year, but I didn't stay long because it was too damn depressing.

I sit down on the rock beach, watching her walk up to the water's edge.

She turns around and stares at me. "Will you tell me about it?"

I push back the disappointment that just seeing the place wasn't enough for her to remember. "Sure."

She sits next to me, stretching my sweatshirt over her legs. I could make a fire, but I think we'll be leaving right after I tell her this story.

"I took you up here, proposed, and you said yes."

She sighs, knocking her knee to mine. "C'mon."

"I just told you what happened."

"Adam, please."

I sigh and look out over the water. "I tried to make it seem like it was any other time we hiked up here, although I did suspect you knew it was coming. We'd graduated and most of our friends were going to college. Your parents were preparing to move to Idaho. It was summer, so the hiking trails were more crowded, but I brought you here at dusk, right when the park was supposed to close. I'd been helping out at the park ranger office before going to college, so they were doing me a solid."

She smiles and her head is tilted as though she's enjoying the story.

"Like always, you said we should swim. That day was unseasonably warm, but I didn't want you to swim because I wanted to propose first and not when you were wet, but you tore all your clothes off and jumped in."

"I did not!" She laughs.

"You did."

"I ruined your plans."

I glance over and she's frowning. I shake my head. "No, you would've only ruined them if you said no."

"Did you think there was a chance I would say no?"

I look at her again. "No. I was more worried about making it special than I was that you would turn me down."

She puts her hand over her heart. "Go on."

"I set up a tent while you were swimming, and when you were done, I wrapped you in a towel and started a small fire. You nestled between my legs. When the sun was dipping down behind the mountains, I reached into my bag and brought the ring around to you. I like to think I surprised you then. Like you'd expected me to get down on bended knee and stuff, but I guess we'll never know now."

"And I said yes?"

I chuckle. "You said yes."

"And we made good use of the tent?"

I chuckle again. "Yes, very good use. One of the poles ended up breaking and it collapsed on us in the morning."

"I like that," she says.

"We were quite a couple." I stare at the crystal blue water and the mountains surrounding it, thinking about how much has changed in my life since that day but how this scene looks exactly the same.

"I feel it," she says in a soft voice.

My gaze shoots to her and I find her rubbing her chest.

"I feel the love." A tear trickles down her cheek. "I want you to know that. If all of this is for naught, I do love you. It's one thing I'm certain I do know."

I nod and swallow the painful lump in my throat.

"I'm sorry," she whispers. "I wish I could give you the answer you need."

"Me too."

For the first time since she arrived in town, I realize that because of her lack of memory, we're on the same path of discovery—both of us wanting the exact same thing. The problem is achieving it will most likely put a fork on the path—for her to go one way and me the other.

Chapter Thirteen

Lucy

Saturday morning, I finish packing my bag and bring it downstairs to the reception area of the inn.

Mandi's behind the desk and she smiles at me. "Ready to go home?"

"I am, but don't let Adam hear you say home."

She frowns. "He's running late. Got called in last minute to assist with something at work. How about breakfast?" She steps away from the welcome stand.

Mandi still has red hair and curves, exactly as I remember. Though I haven't caught a glimpse of her mischievous smile yet, I'm sure that probably hasn't changed either.

"Oh, he didn't call me."

She tilts her head. "He didn't? Does he not have your number?"

"He does."

Her hand runs down my back. "You know Adam. He probably wanted to make sure I took care of you."

"Yeah. Sure." We both know that's not the case.

Two days ago when he took me to where he proposed, or what I gather was more or less our spot, I felt how much it hurt him to do so. He could barely look at me while he told me the story of how he proposed. How I ruined it by running into the water. Between that and what Amy from Twisted Stem said, I'm not sure I like my old self a whole lot. It sounds as though I had a habit of railroading Adam and doing what I wanted, then expecting him to go along with it.

"Come on. Francois made a delicious breakfast this morning. Little soufflés with whatever you want in them." Mandi picks a table by the window that overlooks the bay and sits across from me. "I can join you for a little bit before duty calls."

A waiter comes by and I give him my order for a soufflé.

"So Francois, huh? You have a French chef?"

"His name is Frank, and he's middle-aged and born and bred here in Alaska, but he's just as bossy as a French chef. Or as bossy as I can imagine one being." She laughs. "He's also brilliant in the kitchen. I've had him for three years and I get so many customers who come back every season for him alone."

I love that she talks to me as though I shouldn't already know what she's telling me. Mandi was only a grade ahead of us, so from what I've gathered from the few new memories that have popped up, we were close. I can remember hanging out with her and Chevelle at the Greene's house.

"Be on the lookout for my mom, because she's on a mission to talk to you." She sips the coffee the waiter brought over.

"Really? Why?"

"Because my mom loves you, but she doesn't want to bombard you."

"I'd like to see her again." I always felt very close to Adam's family. I remember that much. "I'm still trying to remember everything. It's weird how I can remember that Adam is my husband, but not how he proposed or our wedding."

"You'll get there. I'm sure of it."

I nod as the waiter brings over my soufflé. It smells and looks delicious. "I see why you keep him."

"Wait until you taste it, then you'll really know." She slides her hand into her pocket. "Hey, let's trade numbers." She pulls out her phone and her thumbs hover over the screen. "What's your number?"

I tell her and she types it in. I hear my phone buzz in my purse a few seconds later.

"There, now you have mine. Nikki really wants to apologize to you by having a girls' night."

"Apologize?" I ask, the soufflé melting in my mouth. I point my fork at the soufflé. "You weren't kidding."

"Heaven, right? For telling the townspeople to stop you and tell you stories. Jed said Fran and her gang were trying to ambush you the other day." She cringes.

I nod. "Yeah. But I don't blame her. She's just trying to help."

"Oh, you should make her pay for it." She laughs.

"Spoken like a true sister," I say, cutting more soufflé and eating it.

Adam steps into the restaurant and I swear you can hear a pin drop. He's in his park ranger uniform, without the hat. His hair is unruly but stylish in that way that I know he's run his hands through it. He shakes a few hands and greets some other guests before making it to our table.

"Here, take my seat. Want some breakfast?" Mandi asks Adam as he slides into her chair.

"Sure. Tell Frank to make me an omelet though."

"You'll get a soufflé like everyone else," she says and walks away.

Adam rolls his eyes. "Sorry I'm late. We had a group of teenagers who thought it was a good idea to grow pot in the woods."

"Ekk," I say.

"You like that?" He eyes my dish.

I stare at the mouthwatering soufflé on my plate. "I do."

"Huh," he says, and his forehead wrinkles a bit.

"What?"

"You never liked eggs before."

"Really? I've been eating them for as long as I remember." What I said repeats in my mind and I chuckle. "Well, I guess for the last three months."

He frowns. "You wouldn't even make me an omelet."

"Oh." Why wouldn't I make my husband an omelet just because I didn't like them?

"I usually made breakfast." He shrugs.

"And what would I eat?"

"You were a yogurt-and-granola girl."

"Huh. That's odd."

He flags down a waiter and orders a coffee. "So, I haven't been by the cabin since the last renters left, but I had a cleaning crew go in early this morning. If we eat breakfast, they should be done by the time we get there. I'll drop you off and head home to shower."

I put my fork down and tilt my head. "What do you mean head home?"

"I live back at my dad's with my brothers, remember?" When I don't say anything, he continues. "I didn't think we should... live together."

I guess I thought we would live together. But he's right.

It's not like we discussed it or anything. "Oh, right, of course not."

Mandi brings over his soufflé and places it in front of him. "Francois made it special for you." She keeps on walking.

"Tell Frank I said thanks."

Her red ponytail swings back and forth as she shakes her head, stopping at a table and asking if they're enjoying their breakfast.

"You love to razz her, huh?"

He takes such a huge bite, he can only nod as his response.

We eat in silence and look at the bay. Lucky for both of us, Adam eats as fast as a sixteen-year-old boy. Mandi waves off the bill and Adam picks up my bag on the way out, then deposits it in the back of the truck.

While he's pulling out of the lot, my stomach erupts in a fit of emerging butterflies, hoping that physically being in our house, the place where we were husband and wife, will spur something out of the darkness.

I SUSPECTED we had lived closer to where he works, so when he takes the roads farther up the other side of the bay, I'm not surprised. But the farther we drive, I find myself growing a little uneasy about sleeping here by myself.

He pulls up in front of a gorgeous little house that resembles a log cabin.

"When did we buy it?" I ask.

"Right after the wedding. It's not huge, but it's... was ours."

I hate those stuttering pauses when he talks about our past.

I open the car door and he takes my bag before climbing the steps up to the front door. He unlocks the door and pushes it open for me to go in first. I step in, soaking in the entryway and walking into the great room that has floor-to-ceiling windows overlooking the bay far below. The kitchen is on the right, modern enough that I think maybe we renovated it. There's the couch that was in the flashback I had about his head in my lap and the fire going. I smile that I put those together.

I hear him come in behind me and drop the key on the kitchen counter. "This is yours now."

I glance back, too mesmerized by the view to give the rest of the cabin my full attention. "I see why we loved it."

"Yeah, the view sells the shitty shape it's in. Although I've tried to make some improvements."

"Really? Like what?"

"We were in the middle of the kitchen redo when things ended, so I finished that."

I look closer at the kitchen. It's pretty with white cabinets, marble-looking counters, and stainless appliances. "It looks really nice."

"Thanks." He runs his hands through his dark hair. Then he points down the hall. "The master bedroom is that way, and there are two more bedrooms upstairs."

Walking down the hall, I see there aren't any pictures of us anywhere, which I guess makes sense since he's been renting the place out, but it doesn't make it feel very warm or inviting.

Just like the rest of the house, the bedroom is plain but nice with a queen-size bed and nightstands and dressers. No personal items that speak to the people who live here. It's like four walls and a roof instead of a home.

I return to where he is in the kitchen. "I have some money. Would you like me to pay you for the rent you'll be missing out on?"

He shakes his head and sits on a breakfast stool. "No."

I want to ask him what he did with all of our stuff, but he's back to being closed off. Being here is probably different for him than me. I feel as if I'm in someone else's life, and he's probably remembering when we had sex on every surface because we couldn't get enough of each other.

He stands. "Let me give you something before I go." He heads out the door and returns a minute later, heading straight into the living room. I can't see what he has in his hand but he puts it on the side table by the couch then turns to me. "I need to go. You have my cell if you need to call me. I put a gun in there in case you have a run-in with a bear. And for fuck's sake, don't go running out there alone. Got it?"

"Okay—than—"

He doesn't wait for me to finish. The door slams and his truck roars to life a minute later, then his tires screech out of the driveway.

I sit on the couch and stare out at the view. What the hell am I doing? So far nothing is coming to me. I thought this was going to be the big reveal. Like I'd walk in and magically all my memories would flood back.

The hardest part about this memory thing is that it's like I'm in someone else's life. Strike that—it's like my life ended right after graduation and everything I knew to be true isn't.

I walk around the house, opening up closets and looking under the beds. There has to be something personal here. I just need to find the right trigger to jar this part of my memory free.

The garage has some four-wheelers inside, but that's it. As I'm walking back down the hall, I notice a closet I didn't check. I turn the knob and nothing. There's a deadbolt lock on the door, but I pull again as though I'm expecting a fairy godmother to wave her magic wand and unlock it.

My next mission is getting into that closet. A small part of me is happy there's a chance what I've been searching for is behind that door. If so, then it means that Adam didn't throw our entire relationship away, even if I did. It may end up only being pictures, but at least he didn't destroy them forever.

Chapter Fourteen

Adam

I expect to find an empty house when I pull up at my childhood home, but the driveway is lined with trucks. Great. I quickly debate if I want to reverse and get the hell out of here, but my dad steps out of the house and waves as though he was expecting me.

I park the truck in a spot that should stay clear for me to make an exit should I need to.

"Adam, how are things?" my dad asks, leaning along the railing of the porch.

"What are you doing here?"

"Well, Marla felt you guys live in filth, so she decided today is spring cleaning day."

I turn around to go back to my truck. Last time it was spring cleaning day, I ended up sorer than when I hike five miles. The woman doesn't stop until every dust bunny is dead. I'm not even sure why she goes to so much effort. We're all bachelors here, no one cares.

Rylan, my eleven-year-old half brother, comes outside,

doing that damn *Karate Kid* soccer ball bouncing on his knees thing.

"Hey, Ry guy," I say, stealing the ball from him.

"What's up, Adam?"

"You have soccer today?"

"Tomorrow. You gonna come?"

I ruffle his hair. I can't believe he's almost my height. "I'll see what I can do."

"You should. He's playing Calista's team." My dad puts that inflection in his voice to suggest Rylan likes Calista.

Rylan rolls his eyes and continues bouncing the ball. "We're not even friends."

"You should talk to your brother about finding love young. He found his."

I clasp Rylan on the shoulder. "Trust me, stay clear."

He scowls. "I don't even like her. She thinks she's better than me."

Rylan and Calista have been rivals since they were young, when the coach made them practice together because the two of them are the best competition they have in this area. I hate to break it to him, but he probably does like her. But unlike the rest of my family who razzes the kid every chance they get, I try not to bug him about it too much.

"Is it safe?" I point toward the door.

"She's in the kitchen. Fisher's taking a shower," Rylan says.

I groan and open the screen door.

Jed's carrying a laundry basket full of crap and drops it on the couch. "Cade got off easy when he moved out. He doesn't have to do these spring cleaning days anymore."

"No, but he does have Presley to nag him to death," I say.

Jed laughs and sits on the couch to sort through the stuff.

"Marla, I'm in the shower!" Fisher screams from the bathroom.

We laugh.

"Just stay behind the curtain," my stepmom hollers back. "I can't hear myself think with this music playing."

A minute later, Fisher's music—which he blares during every shower—is turned off.

"And I don't want any excuses, you need to come and help your brothers."

"I could arrest you," Fisher grumbles.

The door opens and Dad and Rylan come back inside. I need to figure out an excuse to get out of here and I need to do it fast.

"Is he playing the arresting card again?" my dad asks.

"He is a sheriff," Jed says.

"He's also my son." My dad goes to the stairs and hollers up, "Get out of the bathroom, Marla."

She comes down, a bandana around her hair and wearing her cleaning jeans and sweatshirt that says Just the Tip. I don't get it, but every time she wears it, Dad can't keep his hands off her. It's gross really. "I was just turning down the music. I couldn't even think."

"It's like when they were teenagers. Hard to believe we only have one who's home right now." My dad's hands slide around her waist and he walks her through the opening that leads to the kitchen.

All of us stare at one another and Rylan gags. "They're like that all the time. Can I just move in here?"

"You should be thankful there's not going to be a little Rylan Junior." Jed's eyebrows raise. "Thank God Hank got fixed after you."

"Fixed?" Rylan looks confused.

I sit on the couch, grinning, and wait for Jed to explain the vasectomy procedure to our younger half brother.

"They cut off your balls," Jed says simply.

The soccer ball drops from Rylan's hands and he squeezes his legs shut. "What?" His eyes are wider than I've ever seen them.

"Relax, they don't cut them off," I say, eyeing a laughing Jed. "They just cut off the route the semen takes so you can't produce a kid."

Rylan's forehead wrinkles. "Semen?"

"Has Hank not given you the birds and the bees talk yet?" Jed asks.

He scowls at Jed. "I know enough."

Jed nods. "Well, semen makes babies. Just remember that. And when you need condoms, go to Fisher."

"Come to me for what?" Fisher comes down in a pair of track pants, pulling a T-shirt on over his tatted chest. He gives me a nod when he sees me.

"Never mind," Rylan grumbles.

Fisher shrugs, grabs his shoes from the front entrance, and sits down.

"Where are you going? If I'm being tortured, your ass is too." Jed abandons the laundry basket on the table and sits back comfortably into the couch.

Rylan sits on the floor, bouncing that damn soccer ball everywhere.

"Cam's coming. I've got an appointment at Smokin' Guns in Lake Starlight."

"Another tattoo?" I ask. Not that I'm against them, but it's like Fisher can't stop.

"Yes, golden boy," Fisher says, tying his shoes. "Another tattoo."

Just then, Cameron's truck pulls up and parks behind mine.

"Why do you call him golden boy?" Rylan asks.

Fisher stands, running his hands through his longer dark strands. Seeing him in street clothes, no one would think he was a sheriff, more like the town delinquent. "Because Adam does everything right. He married the first girl who gave him some. He's a forest ranger, because he loves rules so much—"

"Says the *sheriff*." There was a time I hated him calling me golden boy, but now that we're older, I don't really give a shit.

"Speaking of, where is the lady love?" Jed asks.

Marla laughs coming into the room, my dad's hands on her sides as though he doesn't want her to get away. Rylan groans and looks away. I can't imagine living with those two. They're like teenagers.

"I heard you picked her up from the inn today?" Marla continues picking stuff up from around the room and putting it in the laundry basket.

My dad sits on the edge of the couch Fisher just vacated. How does he get out of spring cleaning day?

"She's at the cabin," I say.

Marla stops and turns to look at me. "Alone?"

All of them look at me, even Fisher at the door.

"Yeah," I say.

"Adam." My dad sounds disappointed in me.

"She's an adult."

"With memory loss. We swore to Susan that we would look after her," he says.

"I didn't swear anything to Susan." I stand, not needing a lecture on how to handle my soon-to-be ex-wife.

"Put Susan aside for a moment," Marla says. "Do we

even know if Lucy remembers how to use a stove? I'm certain she probably doesn't know what to do when she's taking out the trash and a bear or some other animal approaches."

"I left her a gun in the side table in the living room."

"Adam!" Dad shouts.

"What?"

He looks at Marla and they have some private conversation with their eyes that results in Marla pulling out her cell phone and walking out the front door.

"Hey, Greene fam." Cam kisses Marla's cheek and walks into the house. He stops cold and looks around. "Oh, what's the drama?" He rubs his hands together.

Cameron's an only child, so he thrives on the drama of our large family.

"Let's go." Fisher grabs his coat.

"Where are you going?" my dad asks. "It's spring cleaning day."

"I have an appointment," Fisher says. "And Liam is booked for months."

"Sit your ass down." My dad points at the couch. "Liam has a family. I'm sure he understands obligations."

"I'm twenty-fucking-nine, Dad. You don't run my schedule," he says.

Dad looks outside, and when he sees she's still on the phone, he turns back to us. "Marla asks nothing of you boys. Do you know how often the girls come over? All the time. You guys live here, never come by our place, act like you can barely make the Sunday dinners. She's cleaning your whole house today. You damn well can help."

Fisher looks at Cam, who blows out a breath.

"If I agree to go to Sunday dinner, can I leave today?" Fisher asks, desperate to get out of this.

"No."

Cam pats Fisher on the shoulder. "Come on, Fish, it'll be fun."

"And who cleans your house?" Fisher grumbles.

"The housekeeper, of course. That's why I like to be here. I get to roll up my sleeves," Cam jokes, although he does have a housekeeper. That's what happens when your family owns the majority of the fishing boats that come and go out of the port.

"I gotta reschedule then." Fisher disappears through the kitchen.

Marla comes back in. "You should thank your sisters. They're going to go over there tonight to spend time with Lucy, but, Adam, this is your responsibility."

"The hell it is," I say.

"Adam." Dad uses his calm but authoritative voice.

I raise my hands in front of me. "Is everyone forgetting she walked out on me?"

"Did you or did you not take vows that said in sickness and in health? Did you or did you not tell her you would help her? She told Mandi that you were being so great in agreeing to show her places and things to try to help her regain her memory."

"I did." I weave my hand through my hair.

"Then it's your responsibility. Why you thought you could just drop her off and let her fend for herself up there is beyond me."

"I can't live there," I say.

Marla's hand runs up my arm. "I know this is hard and we wish we could take away the pain you're feeling, but there are three bedrooms. No one said you had to sleep with her."

Says the woman who can't stop touching her husband.

Does she know how hard it is to be around Lucy and stop myself from wanting to sleep with her? I might hate her, but my dick says I don't. No matter how hard I try, with the way Lucy keeps looking at me, he's gonna win eventually.

"What do you want me to do?" I ask in exasperation.

"You move in there for the time being." Dad stands.

"This is insane," I grumble.

Jed, Fisher, and Cameron all stand around, not saying a word. Like they're on her side too.

"I thought I was the damn Greene. Shouldn't you guys be on my side?" I yell.

"Technically, she's a Greene too," Jed says.

Fisher and Cameron snicker.

I refrain from telling them to fuck off, and instead go upstairs to pack my shit, wishing I was an only child like Cam.

Chapter Fifteen

Lucy

After searching the entire place for a key to the door and spending some time in each room to see if anything new comes to me, I end up in the kitchen because my stomach won't stop growling. I open the fridge, expecting to see it empty—I figure I'll have to call an Uber or something to take me to town—but it's fully stocked.

Pulling out stuff to make a sandwich, I hear something outside and go still. I don't hear anything else, so I start in on my sandwich again, trying to ease some of my anxiety. Although I love having time by myself, since my accident, I find I'm anxious after too long alone. Mostly because being alone with my thoughts only spurs worries that I might never be who I was.

The knock on the door surprises me and I glance at the side table where Adam said he put the gun.

"It's us!" Cora screams from outside, as though she understands why I would be fearful.

I open the door and find Cora, Nikki, Mandi, and Chevelle on the porch. They hold takeout bags and wine.

"We come bearing gifts," Mandi says.

Cora walks in first and I can tell from how comfortable she is that she's been here plenty.

"You guys don't have to," I say, but one by one, they come in.

I give Chevelle a hug, since this is our first time connecting since I've returned to Sunrise Bay.

"Man, he did a number on this place, huh?" Cora looks around. "Talk about stripping it bare." She sets the takeout on the counter.

"Well," Mandi says, "he's renting it out."

"He took down every picture of you two." Nikki shakes her head. "But Mandi has a point. Even short-term renters don't want to see other people."

I keep telling myself the same thing.

"Where do you think he put it all?" Cora asks, taking small foil-wrapped items out of the bag.

"There's a locked closet. I don't have the key," I say.

Cora drops a foil-covered item on the counter and heads down the hall. We all file behind her as though she has the magic code to open the closet.

She tries the knob like me and nothing. "I bet all your crap is in here."

I nod. "I can't find a key."

Cora taps her finger to her lips. "Let's eat first, then we're going to outsmart that guy."

We all head back into the kitchen, and as they unwrap the foil packets, I see that they brought tacos.

"You used to love only chicken, but we brought a variety just in case," Mandi says as she grabs plates and Nikki gets the silverware.

"Were you guys here a lot?" I ask, watching them move around the kitchen as though it's theirs.

They both stop and look at one another. Nikki says, "You and Adam always had the Super Bowl parties. A lot of Saturdays, it was like an open house here. Adam would always be smoking something."

I jolt in surprise. "*Smoking* something?"

"In the smoker." Mandi points out back toward the deck. "If you go down the stairs, you'll find it."

Curious, I walk out to the deck and see the staircase that leads down to a path toward the firepit. I leave the girls in the house and head down the stairs. I find a big smoker that's chained to the post of the deck with a sign that says it's not for the use of renters. Farther out, there's a firepit dug out with chairs around it to the left of the path. Someone did a lot of work here.

"You okay?" Nikki comes out and puts her hand on my shoulder.

I nod. "Yeah, I just wish I'd remember."

"I'm sorry," she says.

"Don't be."

"I heard you can't go anywhere without people blurting out stories." She cringes.

I laugh. "Yeah, but I know they're just trying to help."

"Oh, phew. Back in the day..." She stops talking. "I'll make amends on Monday."

She rests her head on my shoulder and I lean my head on hers. Just as I do with Adam, I feel a bond with all the Greenes, but I can hardly remember any moments with them. It's a weird feeling.

"Hey, what did you mean by 'back in the day'?"

She picks up her head. "Come on, we need to get back before your favorite tacos are gone." She ventures up the path toward the house. "We should have a fire tonight. I'm sure Adam has firewood around here somewhere." She looks under the deck where the smoker is. "There it is."

"Nikki," I call.

"You know he's got, like, all five-star reviews on this place. Well, except for this one person."

"Nikki," I repeat.

"The woman was a real pain. She called Adam, like, twenty times while she was staying here, and she complained about everything. Three-star reviewed the place saying it was rustic. I mean, what did she expect?"

"*Nikki!*" I yell and she stops talking. "Tell me what you were going to say."

"Nothing. I shouldn't have said anything. Just forget it."

"Seriously, you're going to just leave me hanging?"

Her shoulders deflate like a teenager exhausted by her parents' demands. "I can't. It was nothing."

"Please? Everyone in this town knows me and who I was before the accident. What was I really like?"

"Let me at least get the fire started. I'm the best at it and if the girls upstairs find out what I'm about to tell you, they're going to send me rolling down the mountain." She heads under the deck to get the firewood.

"That's scary." I go over to help her carry all the wood we'll need.

"I'm making it sound bad. It's not really, it's just I swore I wasn't going to say anything."

"Did you hate me?" I drop the wood by the firepit while Nikki carefully stacks hers into a pyramid.

"No, God no. I loved you. Not only as my sister-in-law but as my friend. It was just that you could be..."

I put my hands on my hips and look at her while she's working. "Nikki, spit it out."

"Overbearing?" She sighs and looks away. "This is horrible."

I cover my heart. "Was I a bitch?"

She laughs. "We can all be bitches. You just liked things a certain way and made sure everyone knew it. And all I meant is that before your accident, you would've stomped down to the radio station and more than likely told me off. Deservedly so."

I help her position the wood, and she slides the kindling between the gaps in the wood pyramid she's built. "I sound like a bitch."

"You weren't a bitch. Like, take this right now. The Lucy I knew wouldn't have been helping me."

"What?" My eyebrows draw down.

She nods. "You would've sat in the chair while I did it."

"Man." I grab the lighter and flick it to start the fire. "I'm sorry."

"Don't apologize. I'm making it sound worse than it was. It was just you. No one disliked you for it."

"Hey, you two! You're missing out on some great tacos!" Cora yells over the deck, her mouth still full of food.

"We started without you," Mandi yells down from beside her as she refills Cora's wine glass.

"Come on, let's go have fun and forget me ruining our night." Satisfied that the fire is going enough, Nikki turns to go back up the stairs.

"Nikki," I say.

She glances over her shoulder.

"Do you think Adam loved me? Like, truly loved me?"

"Oh." She comes back and puts her arms around me. "That is one thing I'm certain about. That boy never stopped loving you. This is why I wish my big mouth would just stay shut." She squeezes me. "We all loved you, Lucy. We loved you like you were one of us, and like any family member, we all have annoying tendencies. I hate the way Mandi acts so damn perfect all the time. Or the way Posey gossips at the hair salon and won't share any of it with me. And Cade's judgmental attitude toward my radio show makes me crazy, as does Jed flirting with every female in a ten-foot vicinity. We have our quirks. And you had yours. That's all. It was neither good nor bad. It just was."

She squeezes me tightly again. She might be the best hugger I've come across. Although since the accident, I haven't been hugged that much I guess.

"Now, let's go have tacos and a fun girls' night, okay?" She smiles at me.

"Can I ask one more question?"

She sighs.

"You're the only one willing to be truthful with me."

Her head moves right and left. "Which is probably the quirk none of my family likes about me." She laughs.

"Was I happy? Like, truly happy with Adam?"

Another sigh falls out of her. "I think so. You seemed really happy. But when you left so abruptly, we were all in the dark. Shocked, really."

"I feel like I was too. I want to be with him now, but did I find something out that changed how I felt? What if I was cheating on him?"

She laughs. "In this town? Hmm... I doubt it, but I suppose anything is possible. If you were, where's the guy?"

I nod. "I didn't return to Idaho right away. Maybe me and that guy broke up."

"Then why didn't you come back here?"

"Because I left Adam? I don't know." I shrug.

She rubs her hands down my arms. "I don't think you cheated on him, if that's what you're worried about. You two were always together. And when he was working, if you weren't, you were usually hanging with Cora or one of us Greene girls. You didn't enjoy being alone."

"Well, that hasn't changed."

"Then it's a good thing we bombarded you, huh? See? And they say I don't have good ideas." She laughs.

"Could he have been cheating?" My chest tightens as I wait for her answer.

She shakes her head. "No way. Hell, it took him so long to get over you. Alicia is his first girlfriend and I'm not even sure how long they've been dating. We were just meeting her the night you came back."

My eyes widen. "Really?"

She grins like she's happy to divulge this little piece of information. "My gut says you leaving had nothing to do with a third party, but I've been known to be wrong before. God knows my instincts haven't led me to a good man." She chuckles.

"No boyfriend for you?"

She shakes her head. "I'm going to be a spinster, I know it. Or the aunt who watches all her siblings have their happily ever afters."

"Who's spoken for in the family?"

"Well, Cade has Presley. You and Adam..."

I open my mouth to argue with that.

"Nope, you two will figure this out. I know it. And then Xavier and Clara?"

"Clara Harrison?" I ask.

"You remember?"

I shuffle through some visuals in my mind. "Wait, I noticed that Presley and Clara look a lot alike."

Nikki's eyes widen. "They're long-lost sisters. Long story. I'll fill you in later." She waves it off as though it's no big deal, but now my mind is racing. "So you remember Clara then?"

I nod.

"Well, I think she and Xavier are probably banging behind closed doors. In his off-season, they're always together. So there's them too. And then as much as I hate to say it, a woman will end up being Jed's demise at some point."

"I guarantee you you're going to find the one," I say. "He'll probably be someone you least expect."

She swings her arm around my shoulders. "You know what? I love this new Lucy. Maybe go to Posey for a new hairdo. A pink pixie cut for the new you."

"Was pink my favorite color?" I ask.

She laughs and drops her arm from around me, shaking her head at me at the bottom of the stairs. "Stop asking what was and think about what is. Who cares what your favorite color was? What color is your favorite now? You always did put way too much pressure on yourself."

She climbs the stairs while I stand speechless at the bottom. Maybe she's right. Maybe I need to stop trying so hard to get that Lucy back and just live my new reality— discover who I am now.

"Trouble just walked in," Cora screams out the patio door.

Nikki looks at me from the top of the stairs.

"What?"

"The boys just invaded girls' night," she says.

"Hey, mind eraser." I look up and see Jed leaning over the railing, grinning at me. "Look, the girls can actually make fire."

"Did you use a starter log?" Cade hollers from somewhere on the deck.

Nikki flips them off and heads inside.

By the time I walk up the stairs, only Adam is on the deck. "I see you found everything."

"Except the key to the closet," I say.

He looks away.

"Adam?"

"Tomorrow. Can we please just do it tomorrow? I just want to relax tonight."

"Okay," I agree, not wanting to put a damper on tonight either.

"Really?"

"Yes!" I throw my hands in the air, a little exasperated that no one expects me to give even an inch.

"Did you get a chicken taco already? Because you know those guys will eat them all."

"I think I want a beef one."

A small smile creeps on his face. "Come on, I'll wrestle one away from them for you." He nods toward the house and I follow him.

I still have so many questions I need answered, but for tonight, I'll try to live in the moment.

Chapter Sixteen

"Way to ruin the party, Xavier."
~Cameron Baker

Adam

I watch from across the deck as Lucy eats steak tacos and drinks beer inside. She's chatting with Jed and he's making her laugh. Jed makes most people laugh. He's got a personality that just wins people over. The pull of jealousy threatens to unleash.

I've never felt insecure when it came to Lucy, but that was before she walked out on me. I have no idea how I forgot about that closet. Of course she'd want those journals she'd been writing in forever, though I don't know if she knows that's what's in there.

Even if she does get her memory back, what does that mean for us?

"Come on, have some fun." Cameron puts his arm around my neck and rocks me back and forth.

"Leave him be," Chevelle says as she drinks a glass of wine on her way to the firepit. Everyone is heading down now.

Cameron rolls his eyes, then he leans over the ledge of

the deck and watches my little sister make her way to the firepit. He pushes off the railing and is one stair down when I speak.

"You know she's your best friend's little sister, right?"

He gives me an 'as if' expression. "I just enjoy razzing her. Don't read anything into it."

He jogs down the stairs while I shake my head at him. One of these days, Fisher is gonna punch him in the face for flirting with Chevelle.

We all know that whoever ends up with Chevelle will have a lot of issues to deal with, and the worst possible person for that job would be Cameron. The guy's had everything handed to him on a silver platter his whole life. But I can't worry about them. I have enough of my own damn problems right now.

"Marla made me clean the toilet," Fisher tells Cade as they come out onto the deck, Presley snug under Cade's arm.

"Serves you right. I did it. I can't imagine what it looks like without me there now." Cade shivers.

Presley leaves her fiancé's side, walking toward me. As usual, she looks as if she stepped out of a glamour magazine. She has a face full of makeup and clothes that can't be bought around here.

"Did you know it's a party?" she asks with a tentative smile.

I lean against the railing in the corner. "I did."

"Then why are you over here?"

I eye inside.

"You know he flirts with everyone. He tried to pick me up when I first came to town. Women know he's just a flirt." She sips her wine.

"Well, she's not the Lucy I remember," I say, though I'm

not upset about the fact that she's broadened her horizons on so many things.

"I can't imagine being her. I mean, when I came here, I didn't know my family and I hate that I'll never know what kind of people my parents were, but I can't imagine actually not knowing anything about myself. Things we take for granted. You know?"

"Yeah. I know. She's different in a way but still the same."

She leans with me to look down over the firepit.

"What do you think will be the end result of all this?" I ask. I trust Presley. She was the first one to help me sort through my grief from my failed marriage and a large reason why I came out of my depression.

She holds her wine glass over the edge, clasping both sides, both of our gazes on the trees now. "I don't know. You harbor feelings of abandonment that she doesn't remember the cause of. She remembers she loves you, but not anything specific. What I do know is that love is powerful. It's the one emotion that changes people. You know?"

I chuckle. "No, I don't know."

She laughs as though she's winging this entire conversation. "What I mean is, love is strong enough to make people change."

"You said that," I say, chuckling.

Her shoulders sink. "If someone is happy, they're content to stay that way. If someone is depressed, they might know something has to be done, but the emotion itself isn't what spurs them to act to get out of it. Love for someone else is strong enough to force you to get over your problems, get over your hang-ups, get over the big brick wall that's blocking you from having a future with that person. I'm probably talking nonsense since I'm getting married soon."

"No, I understand."

"The fact that she remembers she loves you, without remembering all the things that led to that feeling, that speaks to the power of the emotion."

"She doesn't remember my proposal," I admit.

"Maybe because she already loved you by then."

I nod a few times. "What if the new Lucy doesn't love the old Adam?" I ask the question that's been keeping me up at night. The one I ask when I admit to myself that maybe I still want a happily ever after with Lucy.

"I thought you were only in this to see why she left you?" She cocks a perfectly arched eyebrow at me.

I shrug. "I'm just speaking in hypotheticals."

"Oh, well in that case, I'd say that old Lucy and old Adam aren't a problem because neither one of you are who you were before she walked out. Even if she regains her memory, she's not going to be the old Lucy anymore. And the old Adam left when the old Lucy walked out on him. Maybe you need to get to know one another again."

"Pres!" Cade calls to her.

She smiles and her hand squeezes my forearm. "Smile, will you? It's a party." She walks over to Cade and he takes her hand, leading her down the steps to the fire.

"Is that Cameron down there with Chevelle?" I hear him ask.

"Just relax," she says.

I turn around and find Lucy inside, cleaning up the taco wrappers and empty beer bottles. She looks up and our eyes catch. She smiles softly and my returned smile makes hers grow wider.

Presley's right. I need to be honest with myself. I still love Lucy, and I don't want to divorce her in two months. But the first thing I have to do is figure out if I love the new Lucy and if she loves me now after all the damage.

Pushing off the deck, I walk into our house, ready to do things differently.

"Where's Brody?" someone on the other side of the firepit asks Cora and Toby.

"At your parents'." Toby laughs and finishes off his beer.

Cora is tucked into Toby's lap. Presley's sitting on Cade's. Everyone else is sprinkled around in their own chairs.

"Why is he at our parents' house?" Nikki asks.

"Because none of you have kids," Toby says.

"You better hurry because Marla is definitely ready." Cora eyes Cade as Presley beams as though maybe that's a possibility.

"Huh," Lucy murmurs. I'm pretty sure I'm the only one who heard her.

"What?" I ask when the conversation turns to Cade and Presley's wedding plans for next year.

She turns to me, and the glow from the fire makes her even more beautiful. It takes me back to gatherings after football games in high school when she'd be in my arms like Cora is in Toby's. I never thought I'd be in the situation we're in.

"Why didn't we have kids?" Lucy asks.

I shrug, not up for this discussion when everyone is here. The old Lucy had a lot of feelings on the subject. "We got married young. I guess we didn't think about it."

I'm lying and her gaze falls down. She turns back toward the fire, accepting my answer but not believing it, I think. She shouldn't. I wanted kids and still do. I want the big family I had growing up, and I thought since we married young, we had the opportunity for that. It was the one argument we had and kept coming back to. She wanted to go for her master's and maybe even her doctorate in education. Having kids would have only delayed that.

The conversation around the fire turns to bachelor and bachelorette parties.

Jed raises his hand. "I say Vegas."

"Of course you would," Nikki says, lowering his arm for him.

"Where else is there?" Fisher asks.

"I don't think we're even having them," Cade says. "Neither of us feel the need to have one last night of freedom. We don't see our marriage as a jail sentence."

Presley kisses Cade's cheek, but he puts his finger to her cheek and turns his head, turning the kiss R-rated.

"Hey, you're not alone out here." Nikki throws a marshmallow at him.

"Should we be upset that we weren't invited?" Posey screams from the deck, standing next to Xavier and Clara.

"It was impromptu. We're welcoming Lucy back the right way!" Cameron yells.

The three of them walk down and unfold the chairs they brought, well aware of what happens when we all get together—there are never enough seats.

"I stopped at Mom's and she's watching Brody. She told us you were having a party. And Rylan said he better see every one of us at his soccer game tomorrow." Posey points at each of us. "Hank added even if you're hungover."

We all groan. It's not that we don't love the kid, but we're into football, not soccer.

"The kid should be playing football," Jed says.

"I don't know, have you seen him throw?" Fisher says. "He's got stronger legs than arms."

No one says anything because it's true. Although I think

that's only because Rylan's been playing soccer so long. If there wasn't such a big age gap, I'm sure he would've been a football player like the rest of us.

"It's just as dangerous," Cade chimes in. "And since Rylan has the Greene competitiveness in him, he's gonna end up with a concussion the way he throws his body around."

"Maybe we'll have a pro soccer player *and* a pro football player in our family." Mandi smiles at Xavier. It's his off-season and he stays up here for most of it, spending time with Clara, his best friend. I'm sure I'm not the only one who thinks they're screwing behind closed doors.

"Did everyone see Xavier's passing yards this season?" Clara asks.

"Yes," we all say in unison.

"Oh, Xavier plays the pros?" Lucy asks.

"Yep." I sip my beer.

"That's amazing. What an accomplishment. Congratulations."

Everyone grows quiet.

"Okay, what am I missing?" Lucy asks.

"Nothing," I say.

But everyone's silence speaks louder than my answer.

"Adam?" She looks at me, obviously worried.

"It's nothing."

Everyone's gaze tips down to their drinks or the fire.

"Nikki?" Lucy asks.

I narrow my eyes because that probably means my step-sister has already been a source that's panned out for Lucy in some way.

Nikki sighs. "It's just, um..."

"Nik," I say to get her to stop.

Lucy stands. "Someone tell me."

"Adam had a chance to play," Nikki blurts.

"Nikki," a few of my sisters say, as though she shouldn't have said anything.

"She deserves to know. How would you all like it if you were living in the dark and everyone knew what had happened except you?" Nikki says, and I can't argue with her logic.

Lucy turns toward me. "And I stopped you?"

"I decided not to go. It was my decision." I shrug and look back at the fire.

More silence.

"Why didn't you go?" Lucy asks me.

"Just tell her, Adam," Nikki presses.

I look at Cade and he nods, telling me to go ahead, so I look back at Lucy. "Because you didn't want me to go, but..."

She holds up her hand for me to stop. "Excuse me."

Lucy sprints up the stairs and into the house.

"Way to ruin the party, Xavier," Cameron says, and a few of my siblings laugh.

I follow her because if we're going to move forward in any kind of way, I might as well lay it all out on the table with her.

Chapter Seventeen

Lucy

I rush into the master bedroom, shut the door, and crawl up on the bed. Seriously? What kind of person strips someone's dream away from them?

A soft knock lands on the door. "Luce...y," he says.

"I'm fine. Go back to your family."

The doorknob slowly turns, and he opens the door. "I'm not gonna do that." He steps in and shuts the door. "It's not what you think."

"I took away your chance of playing professional football."

He chuckles. "No. It's not like that."

"That's what they said down there."

He sits on the edge of the bed, far enough away from me that he's not too close, but more intimate than we've been. "I didn't decline the offer because you didn't want me to go." I give him a blank look and he exhales. "Okay, partly, but only because you weren't gonna come with me. Also, it was a chance to play in college, not the NFL. You know how many college athletes actually make it to pro? Not a helluva lot, so there was no sure thing I missed out on."

"But—"

"What's the last memory you've remembered so far?"

"Sixteen. Homecoming." Sadly, I keep waiting for more and nothing comes.

"In that memory you have, we were pretty in love, right?"

I nod against the pillow.

"That love carried through the rest of high school. We were *the* couple. In Nikki's segment, do you remember she called us Cory and Topanga? After the show *Boy Meets World*? We were like every high school sweetheart couple, and I didn't want us to drift apart because we were going to separate colleges." He stands and paces beside the bed. "True, you wouldn't hear about leaving Sunrise Bay. You were going to Anchorage and had decided that you wanted to live the rest of your life in this town."

"And you didn't?"

"I wanted to get out for a while, but I always saw us here in the end. I just thought it'd be fun for us to see what's outside Alaska for a bit."

"I have to say, I have no idea why you loved me, Adam, I sound like a complete nightmare."

He chuckles and sits back down on the bed, taking my hand. My breath hitches when the warmth of his palm meets my skin. "You weren't. I promise. You were maybe a tad selfish at times, but I made the decision to stay here and be a park ranger all on my own. I could have easily told you no. That was a decision *I* made." He squeezes my hand when I don't look up.

"You didn't want to be a park ranger, did you?"

He smiles—a real smile, and God how I love seeing this side of him. I've barely seen it since I returned. The one where all the shit bearing down on us is gone and it's just me and Adam Greene, the boy I've always loved. "I was toying with doing something with my drawing, but I made the right decision. We went to Anchorage for school, me to be a park ranger and to help search-and-rescue on the side. That, along with your job, is what let us buy this place. I love my job. I love being outdoors in nature and how every day is different from the one before. I love getting to save people when they're in trouble. I want you to know I've never regretted that decision. I've never felt resentment toward you."

"Even when I left you?"

"Well. It might've crossed my mind once, but honestly, don't hold any guilt over it. It was a long time ago and we're well past that issue now."

I slide my hands from his and sit up, then wrap my arms around his shoulders. "I'm so sorry," I whisper. "For everything you've been through in the last year. How I could leave you without an explanation seems so heartless. I wish I had the answers you want."

"I should've done this when you first got back into town." He pulls out his keys and slides one key off the chain. He opens my fist and places it inside, closing my fist back up as though this is a journey I'll be going on alone. "Everything in that closet represents our life together, including all your journals. All but the last month of our life together. You must've had a new one at that point and taken it with you."

I hold the key and it feels like a magic bean, full of possibility and weighted with the feeling of freedom. But I don't want to get my hopes up like they were before I came to town. So far, all I've discovered is I was a somewhat selfish person who put her agenda before everyone else's.

"And you should know that I'll be staying here with you. Not here." He looks at the room and a flash of pain strikes his hazel eyes. "But upstairs. My family schooled me pretty bad for not staying with you to begin with."

"Is Alicia going to be okay with that?" Her name feels like poison in my mouth, but I refuse to be as selfish as I sound like I was and just think of myself.

"If we're going to live in truth now, you should know that I broke up with her that day at the diner. We're no longer a couple."

"Oh." I feel guilty for the surge of excitement that swells through me.

"I can't handle this"—he wags his finger between us—"and deal with a new relationship."

"I'm sorry."

"I want those words to stop coming out of your mouth. Well, until you figure out why you'd leave a catch like me. Then you can get on your knees and beg forgiveness." He chuckles and stands. "Seriously though, you need to stop apologizing. You didn't do anything wrong, Lucy. You had an accident and fell off a horse."

He walks toward the door, and when his hand lands on the doorknob, I stop him.

"Thank you, Adam."

He doesn't turn around. "I've always been here for you and that's not going to change now. Then again, depending on what we find out at the end of this, maybe it will." He opens the door and disappears on the other side of it.

ADAM IS STILL SLEEPING when I wake in the morning. His sisters are like their own little cleaning crew. They wouldn't leave last night until the house looked like it did before they came.

I move around the cabin quietly, not wanting to wake him. When I insert the key in the closet and pull the door open, it makes way more noise than I expected and I freeze, looking up and listening. He's done me this solid, and I don't want to cause him more pain by having him look at our wedding photos or whatever else is in here.

When I hear no movement in the bedroom above, I finish opening the door. I release a breath when I see stacked boxes, none of them labeled. I pick one up and tiptoe back to the master bedroom. I go back and forth from the closet to the bedroom until I can shut the door and lock the now empty closet.

I open the first box and find a bunch of framed photos. There are a few of the two of us when we were younger. Another one from when we were crowned homecoming king and queen in high school. A few medals and trophies of Adam's. A newspaper clipping of what an athlete Adam Greene was and how Division One schools were bidding on him due to his older brother Xavier already having a killer start at his college.

There are a lot of pictures of Adam's family and one of him and his mom when he was younger. Then I realize these pictures aren't from our house together—these are from his room. His childhood bedroom.

It was right after our high school prom and I'd brought him over the framed picture. Marla and Hank were gone. We were allowed to be in his bedroom but with the door open. Since his parents were gone, he shut the door and we laid on his bed side by side.

He turned to face me, his hand sliding under the hem of my shirt, running back and forth along my bare skin.

"So they say you're the next big football star," I said, reading over the article again from the fall season.

He took it out of my hands and put it next to his bed. "Forget that. We're going to Anchorage." He nuzzled his face in my neck, his hand sliding up my torso toward my breast. "We only have an hour before they get back."

"Are you going to hate me in ten years?" I turned toward him and his hand pulled my body flush against his.

He kissed the tip of my nose. "We've been over this. I want this."

"I can't have you hate me. I'd never be able to live with myself."

"Relax, I'm good. As long as I've got you, I'm happy." He kissed my lips, but I broke off the kiss right away.

"You sure?"

"Yes, now we have fifty-five minutes until they get home." His hand slid up my back and unclasped my bra. "Whoops."

"What if Chevelle or someone comes home?"

"I'm the only one here and since you were so kind to bring over that framed picture of us, it's my responsibility to give you a proper Greene thank you." His lips found my collarbone, and for a moment, I lost myself in his intoxicating touch.

"Is this the way all the Greenes say thank you?"

He chuckled into my skin on the way down to my breasts. "Only to special people." He peeked up through his eyelashes. "In case you're wondering, you're the most special of them all."

I laughed until he flipped open the button on my jeans. Then he rose on his knees and I opened my legs wider.

Since we'd first had sex after prom, there'd been no more making out, no more stopping at second base. Hell, we never even stopped at third unless I was giving him a blow job.

He shimmied my pants down my body with my help and lit up looking over me, as though he couldn't believe I was his. As *though I was the last Christmas gift under the tree—the one he'd asked for hundreds of times but never thought he'd get. I was addicted to that look, drunk on the fact that I'd somehow found my soul mate when I'd only been thirteen.*

The flashback fades, although I remember how his bed squeaked as he pushed inside me after putting on a condom. The way he was so gentle and sweet and loving. The way we fumbled through movements like an unchoreographed dance. Nothing fluid with motion, but a lot of "hold on," "I got it," "oh wait," "maybe we need to." But that was also the fun. Us finding our groove together. Teenage exploration at its best.

A knock interrupts my memory and I shove everything in the box, rise from the bed, and inch open the door.

"Just seeing if you were up." Adam's wearing shorts and a T-shirt that hugs the muscles in his chest and arms. "Want me to make you an egg since you like them now?"

"Sure."

I open the door wider and he peeks in, his grin turning to a frown for a moment. "I see you found the boxes?"

"I did. Thank you."

I should tell him that one box brought back a memory, but I hold back that information. I feel as though I'm slowly torturing him on some level by making him relive our life—the same one I chose to walk away from.

So instead, I smile and follow him to the kitchen, where I help him make eggs for what I think is the first time. I have no idea why my old self had such a problem doing this because I enjoy cooking with Adam. Especially when I get cocky and think I can crack the egg over the pan instead of the bowl and end up with more shell than egg.

Because he laughs.

And Adam's got a great laugh. I hope I appreciated it then as much as I do now.

Chapter Eighteen

Adam

A week after I moved back into the cabin, I wake up in my spare room and instead of going downstairs, I sit on the edge of the bed for a moment and stare out the front window. The noises downstairs must be from Lucy making breakfast. She's been trying different foods this week. Since she loved Frank's soufflé at the inn, she's "rechecking her palette," as she likes to say. I chuckle. The old Lucy never tried anything she didn't already know she liked.

The same question that's been plaguing me for the past week resurfaces—how can she be the old Lucy but be so different at the same time?

Along with testing every food she can get her hands on, she's been reading her journals and looking at pictures, but if any more memories have come back, she hasn't told me. Still, last night I pulled in the driveway and stood outside the house, looking at the lights glowing from within.

Knowing she was in there tugged at my heart like it was warning me, "you're invested now." Sadly, my heart is right.

I knew when I agreed to help her, the line separating us would get hazy and blurred. But instead of yearning for the old Lucy to return, I'm enjoying getting to know the new one.

I shrug on a shirt and head downstairs to eat breakfast. I've made an appointment with her old principal to bring her in early this afternoon to visit her old classroom and kids. Principal Richards said all the kids have cards and are eager to see her, so I think that will make her happy.

"Oh damn," Lucy says as I enter the kitchen, putting her finger in her mouth.

"Pancake day?"

She nods with her finger still in her mouth. I pull at her wrist and lead her over to the sink, where I turn on the cold water.

"I want to see which fruit I like on my pancakes," she says.

I glance at the counter to see strawberries, blueberries, bananas, and raspberries.

"Don't tell me what I used to like," she rushes out, and I chuckle.

"Doesn't look bad." I turn off the faucet. "Watch it for a blister though."

"It was just the butter on the pan."

"Want me to?" I say, reaching for the spatula.

"No way. You sit and I'll feed you." She points at the breakfast stool.

She's wearing a pair of pajama pants and a T-shirt that reads, "I had amnesia once, possibly twice. Maybe three times. (I don't exactly remember having it)!"

Her vision follows mine down to her shirt. "Oh, Zane got it for me. He thinks it's funny."

I grab a cup of coffee and sit on a breakfast stool. watching her. "And did Susan think it was funny?"

She chuckles. "What do you think?"

"My guess is no."

"Give the man his prize." She points the spatula at me as though it's a magic wand and she's the fairy godmother.

"Have you talked with her?"

She shrugs. "She texted me and I texted back that I'm fine."

"Did you tell her you were here?"

She flips the pancakes and doesn't say anything for a moment. "No. I'm not sure she'd understand." She stacks the finished pancakes on a plate and turns off the stove.

"Did you remember how to do all that? Like how to use a stove and drive a car and things like that?"

She hands me a plate. "Yeah. The technical term is retrograde amnesia. So I remember things before the accident, but my doctor said usually in cases like mine, my memories closer to the accident are less likely to come back. That's why I remembered my parents and you, although there's still so much missing." She frowns with disappointment.

"Have you driven a car yet?"

She laughs and serves me four pancakes before putting two on her plate. "I was with Susan, remember?"

I chuckle. "Well, maybe we can change that."

She glances outside. "I'm not driving from here though."

I coat my pancakes with butter and syrup, no fruit. "I'll be right next to you."

"Next to me while we drive off a cliff." She cuts her pancakes in half, positions the four pieces separately on her plate, and tops each with a different fruit.

"That's what guardrails are for." I wink.

She chuckles then stares at her plate. "Should we wager on which one is my favorite?"

"I'll go with strawberries."

"I'm going with banana," she counters, cutting up the one with blueberries first.

"You know I might have an inside track on this."

She shakes her head. "If you would've bet me last week if I liked that soufflé, you would've said no, so you actually don't."

"Touché." I nod at her to start eating.

I cut a forkful from my stack and pile it into my mouth, wishing we had some bacon. But I'm too lazy to actually make it, and I'm enjoying the game Lucy's playing with herself.

She chews then suddenly stops. "It just burst in my mouth." She laughs, her teeth blue.

I pick up a blueberry from the bowl and pop it in my mouth. "That's the best part."

"Not for me. Although I do like the taste."

"Maybe try a muffin tomorrow."

"Good idea." She points at me with her fork right before she digs into her strawberry pancake. "Hmm..." She swallows. "I did enjoy that one."

I wink because it'll be the winner in the end.

"Now for the one that's actually going to be the winner."

"Hey now, you keep talking like that and I'm going to make an argument about you not being fair with your decision."

Her laughter rings through the entire downstairs. I swear it's still the best sound I've ever heard. When we had the impromptu party over here last week, she laughed too, but not when it was just the two of us.

She puts the banana pancake in her mouth and looks at the ceiling. "It's okay. I like it, but it's not my favorite."

I grin.

"See? I didn't lie. Technically you're the winner so far."

"And what do I win?" My voice is filled with innuendo I didn't intend.

The room quiets and she stops moving. I'm not sure either of us can pretend that our thoughts haven't lingered on sexual ones at times. I've caught her looking at me as if she wants to climb me, and every morning, I have to see her wearing no bra under a thin T-shirt. It takes every ounce of my willpower not to corner her and show her how the sex was between us.

"If you win, I'll drive today," she says.

"Deal," I say, eager to get the thought of screwing her on this counter and eating blueberries and strawberries off her body out of my head.

"Okay then, last one." She puts the pancake with raspberries in her mouth, chews once, and heads over to the sink, spitting it out. "I can't do it. All these little things exploded in my mouth."

I laugh and finish off the rest of my pancakes. "So is it safe to say I win?"

Turning around, she plucks a paper towel off the rack and wipes her mouth. "I always loved strawberries?" she asks, seeming a little disappointed.

I amp up the suspense by shaking my head.

"What was my old favorite?"

I point at the banana and she smiles. But the smile is bright and wide as though she would've been disappointed if she'd chosen the same fruit she used to like.

I knew what Nikki told her at the party was too much. Now Lucy is harboring guilt and thinking she doesn't like the person she was, but I loved that woman. So I vow to myself that I'll make sure she loves that version of herself too, whether or not she ever fully comes back to me.

WE SIT in my truck and she looks way too tiny to be in the driver's seat. When she lived here, she had a small SUV and refused to ever drive my truck. But new times call for new things.

"Do I need to go over the brake and the gas?" I ask.

She shoots me a look to say 'stop it.'

I hold up my hands. "Sorry, but you don't even remember marrying me. I have to make sure we're all safe on this expedition."

She rolls her eyes. "Let's remember this is your idea and I *do* remember marrying you, just not the actual ceremony." She stares at the dash as though she's expecting it to turn on by itself.

"Put the key in the ignition and turn it forward," I instruct her.

"I know. I know." She wiggles her ass in the seat and her back straightens, then she checks her mirrors for the millionth time. I even turned the truck around so she wouldn't have to back down the driveway.

I wait with one arm stretched out across the seat and resting on the back of her seat, my other arm relaxed along the door. "Let's go. We don't wanna be late."

She gives me one more death glare and puts the truck in gear, easing off the brake but slamming it down before we reach the end of the driveway. She cringes. "Sorry."

"No problem."

She leans forward over the wheel to look right and left from our driveway.

Eventually I do the same and she playfully swats me. "I think we're clear," I say.

She eases out and turns the wheel like a brand-new driver.

"Should we see if you can get us to the school?" I ask.

"I know my way."

I hold up my hands and let her take control. Once we're out of the mountains and she's heading toward downtown, she relaxes in the seat and her hands aren't at ten and two any longer. More like three and nine, but it's progress. Other than being heavy on the brake, she's doing great.

"This is fun. I'm gonna have to buy a car."

"Where's your SUV?" I ask.

"In Idaho."

So she drove there at some point. "Why not go down and drive it back up here?"

She shrugs.

"What's with the shrug?" I shift in my seat a bit to face her.

"I think I want to start fresh. I've thought a lot about it, and don't get me wrong." She turns my way and I point toward the road. "I want to remember the reason I left, and I'm going to do everything I can to figure it out, don't think I'm not. But I'm enjoying discovering this new Lucy. How many people get to reinvent themselves?" She pulls up to the school, where they've changed the sign out front to welcome her back. "Oh, look at that."

While she parks, backing up and straightening out a few times, her words strike me again. She somehow doesn't like who she was.

We climb out of the truck and she hip-checks me. "I

don't get a congratulations for remembering how to get to school?"

"Congratulations," I say, smiling at her.

She tilts her head as I press the buzzer to be let into the school. "Are you okay?"

I nod and look straight into her blue eyes. "You know that you were a great person before the accident, right? I wouldn't have fallen in love with someone who wasn't."

She loses her smile for the first time all morning and nods. "I know. I'm just having fun."

She might be a new version of herself, but one thing hasn't changed—I can still tell when she's lying.

Chapter Nineteen

Lucy

Principal Richards and the entire office staff welcome me back with hugs and well wishes.

After our initial hello, Principal Richards and I walk down the school hallway, Adam in tow but keeping his distance, allowing me to rediscover this side of my life without him chiming in.

"So, obviously, your actual class has moved up a grade, but this was your old classroom. We did some swapping and brought in your old class to help you along, see if it triggers any memories." She smiles as though this is a gift. I appreciate her efforts, but in truth, it just feels like more pressure on me.

Adam leans along the wall as the principal knocks and enters the room, telling the kids she has a surprise. She dodges the questions about why they're in their old classroom and who's here and what's going to happen to lunch and will they still have recess.

I chuckle as Adam shakes his head. "Wouldn't it be nice to have the worries of a kid again?"

"Absolutely." I smile at him.

"Here's your surprise. Mrs. Greene is here." Principal Richards holds out her arm as though I'm a celebrity the kids worship.

I enter, apprehensive I'll even recollect how to behave with a class full of children. Was I funny, mean, or serious all the time? I still remember my second grade teacher, Mrs. Phillips, and I hated her.

The class rushes up from the carpet and runs at me, swarming my waist with such a force I almost fall back.

"Looks like they must have liked you," Adam says, leaning against a wall. His raised eyebrows make it clear what he's thinking. I've always been translucent to him—he's able to see right through me.

The kids all fire out questions in unison.

"How are you?"

"My mom said you don't know who you are?"

"You left us, and we had a mean sub."

I field the questions as much as I can, but Principal Richards tries to calm them and tell them not to stress me out. Then a little girl asks what stress means. I hate when people feel as though they have to be my protector when I can manage just fine.

"Let's sit and I'll tell you a little about what happened to me, okay?" I say.

They all listen, sitting down and crossing their legs on the rug.

"Here, we have a chair for you," the teacher of the class says.

"Thanks, Abby," I say, and she freezes.

"You remember me?" she asks with wide eyes and a smile.

I look at her again and nod. "I do." Then my gaze shifts to Adam and he smiles. "Did I meet you after I was married?"

She laughs. "You did. My husband moved up here to work at Bailey Lumber and that's when I started teaching here."

I release a breath. Maybe this whole immersing myself thing is working.

"You and Abby used to do lunch every day," Principal Richards informs me. "You two were always pairing up with special events around the school."

"It's great to see you," I say.

"You look great and..." She glances at Adam. "I'm happy you've returned."

"Me too."

A little girl in the front row raises her hand. She's cute, with two braids, a matching skirt and top, and a name tag that reads Kayla. "Mrs. Greene?"

"Yes."

"Is my mommy right? Do you know who you are?"

I giggle and sit in the chair Abby put out for me. "Let me start from the beginning. Three months ago, I fell off a horse and hit my head really hard."

"I fell off my bike last summer, hurt my wrist," the boy with Logan on his name tag says. I can only assume the name tags were put on them with the hopes it would either trigger my memory or just make things easier on me.

"Children—" Principal Richards tries to step in.

I raise my hand that it's okay. "It's similar to falling off your bike, but horses are really high, so when I fell, I had a long way to go until I hit the ground."

"That's scary," Kayla says.

"Horses are pretty. We have two," Gia says.

"No one cares about your horses, Gia," Evan says next to her.

She sneers at him, giving a look she'll no doubt perfect over the years. I laugh on the inside.

"So I did forget some things, but I do know that I'm Lucy..." My gaze lands on Adam. Do I say Greene or Davis?

"Greene, Mrs. Greene. Your last name is Greene," Kayla says, trying to be helpful, and the rest of the kids groan. "You don't remember, do you?"

Adam shakes his head, trying to hold in a laugh, and slides into a chair at the desk.

"No, I do remember, but you guys know Greene is my married name, right?"

"Yeah, you're married to Mr. Adam and he's a park ranger," Logan says. "I want to be a park ranger."

Adam leans forward and high fives the kid.

"You had him come in and tell us about his job. Don't you remember?" Kayla asks. She seems to be the one most concerned about my memory.

"Can he tell us the story of how he had to scale a mountain to save a man who had no business being up there?" Evan turns toward Adam.

I stifle my own chuckle, assuming that last part must've been Adam's own words.

"Later, bud," Adam says. "Let's listen to Mrs. Greene right now."

Evan turns back toward me.

"I guess you guys really enjoyed Mr. Adam, huh?"

"She doesn't remember?" Kayla looks at Abby with wide eyes like Abby should be picking up the phone and calling 911.

Abby lowers her hands. "Relax. Mrs. Greene is trying to tell a story and you guys keep interrupting. Interrupting is terribly rude, remember?"

"I remember, but does she?" Kayla points at me.

My gaze lingers on Adam behind them and he nods for me to continue and disregard anything they say.

"Anyway, so I came back up here with the hopes that my memory returns."

"And that's why you left us right before the class concert?" Evan asks.

Principal Richards groans. "We discussed this before Mrs. Greene came in, Evan."

"Unfortunately, Evan, that's one of the memories that hasn't come back yet."

"My mommy said that Mr. Adam was really sad. I saw him at the store after you left and he was really nice, gave me a high five." Kayla turns to him. Adam nods that he remembers. "Mommy said if it was her, she'd have a grocery cart full of ice cream and cookies. And I asked why. She said he was nursing a broken heart." She shrugs. "I guess that fixes it." She turns around again. "Did you break your heart too?" she asks me.

I close my eyes briefly.

"How does your heart break?" Evan asks, staring down at his chest.

"Where is our heart?" Gia asks.

"You mean those paper hearts for Valentine's Day?" Logan says.

"My grandpa had a bad heart. Is that the same thing?" Ashley asks.

"Maybe we should just end this," Principal Richards says.

"No, it's okay." I shake my head. "Your heart is right

here." I lay my hand over mine. "The term broken heart is a figure of speech. It means that someone you love hurt you really bad."

"Who hurt Mr. Adam?" Evan stands up as though he's ready to take on the offending party.

"Mrs. Greene did," Kayla answers, pointing at me. I don't remember her, but I'm fairly sure she probably always raised her hand and answered every question.

"Okay, guys." Adam slides out of the desk and comes over to the front of the room. "My heart is fine. I have a great heart. It's healthy and I can still scale mountains to save people." He puts his hand on my shoulder. Other than when he held my hand in our old bedroom a week ago, it's the only time he's touched me. He squeezes.

But the kids aren't saying anything wrong. They're just franker than the adults in this town. Like it or not, everyone in this town thinks I broke Adam Greene.

"Why don't you read them a story now?" Abby hands me a book.

I happily take the book, and the kids allow the distraction to prevent any further talk of whose heart I broke and why. It's still not something I could answer even if I wanted to.

WHEN WE LEAVE AN HOUR LATER, I refuse to drive because my mind is distracted.

"They're just kids," Adam says.

"Their hugs felt good," I say. "I enjoyed being in the classroom with them."

"You were always a great teacher," he says and puts the truck in gear to leave.

"I loved it then?"

He nods. "You did. You'd always come home and tell me stories about what they said. Which you do know..." He glances at me for a second before pulling out on the main road. "Kids say whatever's on their mind. You don't have to worry about what they said."

"I know, but it makes me feel guilty. Maybe if I knew why I left, I'd feel less guilty, or maybe I'd feel even more so. I mean, who knows why I'd leave you?"

He puts his hand on my thigh. A million nerve cells heat under his palm and scream for him to keep it right there, even move up a little. "You have to relax. You have no control over any of this."

I slide my hand over his and link our fingers. "I'm surprised to hear you say that when you're the one I hurt."

"At some point, I have to let the anger and hurt go. I have to find forgiveness."

"Do you think you ever could?" I'm pretty sure I stop breathing as I wait for his answer.

He moves his hand and I expect him to slide it away, but he locks our hands together instead. "I'm trying. I really am."

"I appreciate it."

He's quiet for the rest of the trip, but he doesn't release my hand. When we pull up the long driveway to Hank and Marla's house on the hill, my gut twists.

"What're we doing here?" I ask.

"We're having a late lunch with Hank and Marla. I've put her off long enough and she was bummed about missing the party. She's anxious to see you."

I nod, and he parks the truck at the top of the driveway.

"It's only us here. I told the rest of my family they

couldn't come. Plus, it's a weekday, so that only leaves Fisher and maybe Xavier who might be around. So no worries."

"Okay."

I hate to release his hand for fear it won't happen again, but we can't really get out of the truck like that. So I open my door and climb down, staring at the basketball hoop I remember the boys playing when we weren't old enough to drive but still all hung out. Cora and I practically lived here during the summer since they had the pool with the heater and pretty much all the toys everyone wanted.

"Do you think we could go four-wheeling some time?" I ask as we approach the house.

He glances at me while punching in the garage door code on the opener. "Sure. What spurred that?"

"I don't know. I saw these people the other day on a trail and thought it looked really fun."

He chuckles and the door opens. "Done."

"Thank you."

"Do you want it to be everyone or just us?" he asks, stepping inside and waiting for me.

There's a minivan in the garage, along with every sports toy you could imagine, all aligned in some contraption made for sports gear.

"Maybe just us. I might be rusty, and I don't want everyone watching me."

He stops before opening the door that leads inside the house. Since it's a gloomy day outside, it's darker in here. His body is so close to mine, I want to rub against him, but that'd be creepy and unwelcome, I'm sure. "I'm off on Friday if that works."

"Not like I have a ton of plans."

"Then it's a date... er... I mean."

I giggle and hold up my hand. "It's okay. I understand what you mean."

Our eyes lock, and for the briefest second, I think this could be it. Maybe he'll lean in and kiss me.

Instead he pushes open the door and screams, "Marla!"

She comes around the corner, arms out, pushing Adam out of the way and swathing me in the biggest hug. "My Lucy!" She sways us back and forth while Adam shakes his head, walking into the house.

At least Marla loved the old Lucy.

Chapter Twenty

Lucy

Adam eats some veggies and dip while Marla gushes over me.

"You look so beautiful," she says, going to the fridge and taking out items. "They've kept you from me. Afraid I would be too overbearing. I mean, it's like they don't even know me." She rolls her eyes then winks.

Adam shakes his head, chomping down on another carrot with ranch dip.

"I made all your favorites. Cucumber sandwiches." She places a tray on the table. "Pasta salad with my famous Italian dressing." She shoves a bowl into Adam's stomach, and he fumbles to grab it, a carrot hanging out of his mouth. "And caramel brownies." She points toward the counter where there's a tray.

"Lucy's experimenting with her food," Adam says.

I shoot him a glare. "Adam."

"Experimenting?" A crease forms on the bridge of Marla's nose.

"I'm just trying new foods, figuring out what I like. It's not a big deal. This all looks delicious." I give Adam a 'shut the hell up' look behind Marla's back.

"Oh, I could have added something different. You hated pickles. Want to try those now?"

"I hate pickles?"

"And love cucumbers. Sounds crazy, but to each their own." Marla grabs a decorative plate and piles the cucumber sandwiches on it.

Adam reaches into the fridge, takes out a jar, and cracks it open, giving me a visual of how strong his biceps are. Then he places the jar in front of me. "Have at it."

I pick up a fork Marla's taken out for the pasta salad and grab a pickle out of the jar. "What didn't I like?"

Adam shrugs. "You've never liked them since I've known you."

I eat one, and the tart acidic taste of vinegar with the pickle tastes good to me. I take another bite.

Adam's eyes widen. "Looks like another taste bud changed with that fall off the horse."

"You like it? She likes it?" Marla glances over her shoulder from the sink.

"Lucy likes it," Adam says in the same manner of that old commercial about Mikey liking it.

I roll my eyes, but it is funny. "Please don't start that."

He grins. "I like pickles, so I'm glad you've seen the light."

I hold the one I just plucked out of the jar out to him in case he wants one.

He laughs, directing my wrist to bring the pickle to his mouth, then bites the end off it. "Guess we'll keep them in the fridge at home."

It isn't until I catch Marla staring at us that I realize how instinctual what we just did was.

Adam must realize it afterward too because he goes back to his veggies and dip and clears his throat. "Where's Dad?"

"He'll be here soon. He's out doing some bids, but promised he'd take a lunch break."

She opens the screen door, revealing the table she's set out back for lunch. Only in Alaska. It's an unseasonably mild spring day, but if we were in the lower forty-eight, they'd probably balk at eating outside in this weather. But I remember that you only get so many months of decent weather in Alaska and you enjoy every last bit of it you can.

"I have lemonade, or soda, or anything you want. Show her, Adam." Marla begins taking the food outside.

"Want to play hot or cold?" Adam asks. "You search and I'll tell you if you're close to the drink fridge?"

"Joke's on you, I remember." I stick my tongue out at him playfully.

"Well then." He holds out his arm. "By all means, lead the way."

I head into the laundry room where there's a fridge that holds all the drinks—unless they're having a party, then you usually find desserts in it.

"Smart girl," Adam says, following me into the laundry room.

Rylan's soccer uniform is hanging on the dryer rack. I didn't go with everyone to watch his game last week, opting to stay behind and go through one of the boxes from the closet. "Can I go to one of Rylan's games?"

"Sure. The kid plays all the damn time. He's playing all weekend."

"Great. Let me know where and when?"

"I can take you," he says, opening the fridge door.

"Oh, thanks. I didn't want to assume."

He hems and haws. "It's fine. I told you I'd see you through this process. Now." He holds open the fridge door. "Pick your poison."

You'd think the Greenes owned a soda business with the selection in there. I grab a diet soda and Adam slides by me, cornering me against the wall and the door of the fridge. He reaches in and grabs a sports drink. "Sorry."

"It's okay," I say, a little breathless.

He's so gorgeous. Those hazel eyes pierce mine with the questions I find myself up at night debating. Can we get over this threshold? Can we ever be Adam and Lucy Greene again? What if I never find out what spurred my leaving? What if he can never forgive me? And the biggest question —do I want him to forgive me?

He doesn't allow the fridge door to shut but stands straighter, his free hand falling to my face, his thumb lightly finding my lip. "Marla's right, you look really beautiful today."

"Thank you."

"Luce...y," he says.

The moment fades when he adds the "y" to my name. As if I'm a stranger.

"We should get back." I slide by him and out of the laundry room, trying to calm the flush that's overheating my body.

When I reach the kitchen, I find Hank and Marla kissing by the sink. She's swatting him away, but his lips keep finding skin to kiss.

"The kids," she says with a chuckle.

"Yeah, Hank, the kids," Adam says and walks right by me, paying me no attention.

Hank turns and gives his son a scolding look. Then he turns his attention to me. "Lucy, it's great to have you."

"Thank you."

He comes over and kisses my cheek in hello.

"You two hold down the fort. I just have one thing to show Lucy before lunch." Marla takes my hand.

"Marla, you promised," Hank says.

She shushes him with her hand.

"What?" Adam asks.

Hank groans. "You know Marla."

But I'm already being rushed upstairs before I can hear the rest of their conversation. She gets me into what's now a spare room, but I remember it used to be Nikki and Mandi's. And hanging by the closet is a giant white dress—a wedding dress. I gasp.

"You remember?" Marla looks so hopeful.

My shoulders sink. "No, I just figured if you're showing me a wedding dress that it'd be mine unless you and Mr. Greene are renewing your vows. And in that case the dress might be a little overboard."

She laughs and stands next to me. "You always were funny."

"I was?" I turn to her.

"Yes."

That's one good quality, I guess.

"Now." She heads over to the bed, picks up the veil, and positions it on my head before I have an opportunity to object.

I look at my reflection in the mirror and feel something oddly familiar about this situation. Like every other memory that's come back, it flickers to life and I'm right there, reliving the moment.

"You're gorgeous," Marla said, pinning my veil in place. "Isn't she, girls?"

I was staring at my reflection when Nikki came to my side, smiling. "You are. Adam's going to die. Let's hope you make it to the reception."

"Nikki," Marla scolded.

"They're gonna be married, Mom. You can't be that naive." Nikki sat on the bed, putting on her heels.

The bridesmaids' dresses were a bluish-green, but every girl wore a different style. Mandi didn't want hers as revealing as Nikki's, and Hank hadn't been happy with Chevelle's first choice, insisting the slit was too high.

I watched them all stand there behind me, looking at me, and I was so happy they were going to be my family. My parents had refused to come back from Idaho and said I shouldn't be marrying into the Greene family. They were people who took from others.

I'd grown up in Sunrise Bay, so I knew that when Hank and Marla got together, it wasn't brushed under the rug. Marla was Hank's cousin's ex-wife. She'd returned to town after Jeff Greene cheated on her, and she and Hank rekindled a relationship they'd had when they were in their senior year of high school. Marla had told me it happened fast, and that she quickly knew Hank was the man she wanted to spend the rest of her life with. She'd told me that story when I came to her crying that my family wouldn't agree to me getting married. They thought I was too young and didn't know what I wanted.

Happiness radiated from me that Adam was my future. I turned away from the mirror and allowed everyone to ahh over my dress.

Hank knocked on the door and stood outside the room in a tuxedo. "Ready, ladies?"

"We're ready," Marla said, looking back at me to make sure.

I nodded.

"Good. The boys will meet us there."

Tires squealed out of their driveway—the groomsmen, who consisted of all the Greene men, along with Toby.

"Fucking Toby. We'll be lucky if Adam gets there alive." Cora rolled her eyes.

"They'll be fine," Marla assured me.

We all went down the stairs, through the Greenes' big house, and out to the cars that would take us to the spot where we were to get married. Adam and I had toyed with the idea of eloping somewhere, but I'd wanted everyone to witness me marrying the love of my life. So Adam had found the perfect spot since he'd been working at the park ranger office.

"Not too far in that your dress will get dirty, but far enough that we won't have spectators," he'd said.

I sat in the back of a rented limo with Marla and Hank and Cora. The rest of the bridesmaids were in another car. Cora smiled at me.

Marla took my hand. "Hank and I would like to give you one last thing you need before you get married. Something old."

"Oh." I hadn't been worried about that superstition, but it seemed important to Marla.

"Adam's mom received quite the jewelry collection when her mom passed. The collection has been passed down for generations. Chevelle's already picked out what she wants, and each of the boys picked out the items they'd like to give their significant others once they marry," Hank said.

"Really?" Adam hadn't said anything. It must've hurt him to go through things his mother loved.

"Well, we didn't expect to be at that stage yet, but here we are. Fate is fate." Hank smiled and pulled a small box out of his pocket. He cleared his throat. "Adam would like you to wear this on the way down the aisle."

Hank opened the box, revealing a sapphire stone surrounded by diamonds nestled inside.

"Holy shit!" Cora exclaimed next to Hank. "That's huge."

Hank laughed, familiar with my best friend's lack of a filter.

Marla took the necklace from the box and held it out in front of me. "May I?"

Tears stung my eyes, but I tried to push them back because I didn't want to ruin my makeup. "Please."

She removed the necklace I'd bought from the bridal store. It wasn't a sentimental piece anyway. My hair had been styled up, so she easily clasped the necklace for me. My thumb and forefinger held the sapphire while I felt the rough edges and smoothness of the jewel.

Hank stared at it around my neck for a moment, then he relaxed in his seat and stared out the window. Marla squeezed his knee as though she understood what this moment meant to him. Then he grabbed her hand and smiled at her.

When we reached the area Adam had picked, it was covered in peonies. The sky had been glowing with pinks and blues. Since we couldn't have candles, we'd opted to have battery-operated ones, but the effect was the same.

"Let's get you married." Marla kissed my cheek and rushed up the flower petal path toward where the ceremony would take place.

I caught a glimpse of Jed, who'd been holding out his arm and waiting to walk his mom down to her seat. The rest of the groomsmen and bridesmaids then lined up and walked down the aisle.

Toby and Cora walked up the aisle, leaving only me and Hank.

Hank held out his arm. "I know you wish it was your father walking you down the aisle, but I want you to know how honored I am to give you to my son. Marla and I are both ecstatic that you've chosen Adam to be your husband."

"Thank you," I said and tried not to cry before I reached Adam.

"Laurie would have loved you. I like to think she's smiling down on us today." He nodded a few times as though he was fighting his own tears. "Let's make you an official part of the family, shall we?"

"Sounds great."

We walked down the aisle, and at the clearing, Adam was standing in the middle of a flower petal circle, right at the edge of a cliff. I didn't see the guests in the white chairs or anyone else standing at the front. All I could see was him and his giant smile. His gaze had shifted to the necklace for a brief moment and his smile had grown. He mouthed he loved me, and my heart could've burst into confetti I was so happy.

"You remembered?" Marla's voice drags me out of the memory.

I close my eyes to make sure I wasn't daydreaming. "The necklace." I cover my neck with my hand. "What did I do with it?"

Marla shrugs. "I don't know, sweetie. Just be happy you remembered. I hope you forgive me for being pushy. I just felt like if you saw the dress or the room, it might help. If not today, another day."

I wrap my arms around her and squeeze tightly. "Thank you, Marla. Thank you so much."

This is the most precious memory to come back to me. The only problem with the memory is that I could feel in my bones how happy I was, and it doesn't make sense that five years later I walked out on him.

I really hope I didn't lose that necklace or get rid of it in anger. I hope it's in one of the boxes at the house. I couldn't have been that careless with something that meant so much to him. I know I never would be now, but would the old Lucy?

Adam

Friday morning, I've decided on a trail for us to go four-wheeling and gotten the trailer and the four-wheeler out of the garage.

Lucy's been a little off since Monday when we went to Marla and Dad's. She was so happy she remembered our wedding day, but still... something about her demeanor seems different since then. I thanked Marla even if at the time I thought she was being pushy.

I love Marla. She's never tried to replace my mom, but still finds a way to guide me like a mom. I should've trusted her instincts.

When I walk into the house, Lucy's dressed and sitting at the table, spinning her phone.

"What's up?"

She looks up and grabs her phone, standing. "Nothing, just waiting on you."

"You were thinking pretty hard there."

"My mom," she says. That gives me all the answer I need.

Susan texts or calls daily. Sometimes Lucy talks to her and other times, if I'm in the room, she always ignores her, which I hate. I can't help but think Lucy's trying to hide the fact that we're living under the same roof again.

Although nothing has happened—my blue balls are proof of that. I might beat off every night thinking of the woman in bed downstairs, but I haven't laid a finger on her. When we were at Marla and Dad's, I thought about it for a moment in the laundry room. But if I kiss her, I know she'll have expectations, and I don't know if I can promise her what she wants.

"What did she say?" I ask.

"I was asking her about that last journal that's missing. I really want to find it."

"And she doesn't have it?"

"She says no, but if I kept every one from my entire life, why would I not keep the one from right before I left?"

"True." I grab a water and open the bottle, then down a quarter of it in one gulp.

"Hey, Adam?" she says.

"Yeah?" I get the cooler ready with the sandwiches and snacks I made for us to eat midday when we take a break.

"Can we do something today?"

I turn around and place the drinks in the cooler. "Something else, you mean?"

She shakes her head. "No. I mean, can I have one day where we don't talk about my memory or what happened or who I was then and who I am now?"

The toll from the past couple of weeks shows in her body. I wish I'd noticed it sooner. She looks exhausted and stressed. I desert the cooler and walk over to her, placing my hands on her shoulders. Against my better judgment, I pull her to my chest and wrap my arms around her.

Damn it, her body still fits perfectly with mine. Her head's right under my chin and her arms slide around my waist, squeezing me tightly.

"I think it sounds like a great idea," I say softly, running my hand up and down her back, not nearly ready to let her go now that I've given in to temptation.

"God, I needed this." She lays her cheek on my chest. "You always were a great hugger."

I hold her longer than is appropriate, but she's right, this feels so good. By the time we separate, all I want to do is tell her we should spend the day on the couch, holding one another.

"We should go if we're going to make it back by sundown," I say while I finish packing the cooler.

"I'm so excited. Where are we going?"

"Do you..." I stop myself. "You'll see. It's a surprise."

She smiles like she knows I almost slipped and grabs her jacket. "I can't wait to feel that motor between my legs."

I raise my eyebrows.

"You know what I mean."

"If you like motors between your legs so much." I eye her up and down her body, and she shakes her head.

Her cheeks flush and she disappears into the bedroom.

Fuck. Things are changing between us and I'm pretty sure my willpower is gonna say mercy and do what my body and mind both want to do. But where the hell will that leave us?

She comes back out, and we leave the house and climb into the truck. On the road, she hooks up her phone and puts on some grunge music. I side-eye her.

She says, "What? It's my new favorite music."

I nod and laugh. "You don't wanna know what I've been listening to."

"What?" She turns toward me as much as her seat belt lets her.

"Motown." I don't go into the story of why because of our promise not to discuss anything about her leaving or her memory.

"That surprises me. You were always more of a garage band kind of guy. You'd always find these bands I'd never heard of."

"I guess things change." I look at her for a moment and she sighs, relaxing in the seat.

"How about grunge on the way there and Motown on the way back?" she asks.

"I'd say that's a good compromise."

She smiles at me, and again that familiar feeling of what it's like to find happiness around Lucy overwhelms me.

WE'RE HALFWAY down the trail when we stop for lunch on the shore of one of the lakes. The water looks inviting, like glass on top and surrounded by trees, but it'll still be freezing this time of year. Lucy lays out the blanket and I place the cooler between us just to get some space. Having her at my back with her arms around my stomach for the entire ride made it feel as though no time has passed. Except the old Lucy never wanted to go in the mud and the new Lucy pointed for me to go through it. Not that I'm telling her that though. I keep biting my tongue on so many things that have changed about her. It's not good or bad—just different.

"Having fun?" I ask, lying on my side, grabbing a few chips from the bag.

"Yeah. Do you think I might be able to drive a little on the second half?"

I want to put my hand on the back of her neck, pull her to me, and kiss her senseless, but instead I answer. "Sure."

"I'm guessing I never—"

I put my finger to her lips. "We're not talking about that, remember?"

She smiles and picks up a sandwich I made. "Tell me what you've been doing?"

How do I tell her what I've been doing is pining away over her? That my family was worried about me? "Just working really."

"No town gossip?"

I sit up and take my sandwich out of the bag. "Cade and Presley were the biggest town gossip for a while."

"Tell me about her." She sits with her legs crossed.

"She's perfect for him. You know how he was."

She nods. "I remember you two being very different about your mother's death."

"Yeah."

"You always wanted the family. The happily ever after."

I'm surprised. "You remember that?"

She smiles. "Yeah, you were like that from the first time you kissed me. Like you were searching for your future wife."

"And look at what happened." I ball up the plastic bag from the sandwich and stand to get some distance, but she follows me to the water's edge.

We're both quiet for a minute before she speaks. "Do you think you'll ever forgive me?" Her voice is quiet, as if she's scared of how I'll answer.

"I thought we weren't going to talk about this today?" I head back over to the blanket. "We should get going."

"Answer me, please." She stays in place.

"You wanted one day and I'm giving that to you. Let's put that question aside until tomorrow." I pack up the stuff in the cooler.

"So you can think of how to let me down easy?"

I stop what I'm doing and look at her. "You really want to know?"

She nods slowly.

I blow out a breath and tilt my head back as though I need support from above to get through this. And maybe I do. "I can't be mad at you because you don't even remember making the decision to leave. At least I tell myself that every time I'm with you. And I can feel my anger starting to disappear."

A smile slowly lifts the edges of her lips.

"But that scares the crap outta me because one day you'll either remember or the reason you left will return and I'll be left like fucking roadkill on the side of the road again."

She steadies her gaze on the pebbles under her boots. "I wish we had some closure."

I sit on the blanket. "I do too, but even though you've made great progress, we both need to accept the fact you might never remember the reason why you left."

She approaches slowly as though I'm a wild animal she might startle. Then she lowers herself to the blanket. "Are we fooling ourselves?"

I wrap my arms around my propped up knees. "How so?"

"If this accident has proved anything, it's that playing games and ignoring the problem is a waste of time. Time is so precious."

"Okay, so say it then. Are we fooling ourselves about what?"

"That we can get back to who we were. I know I'm the one who only remembers the good between us. But I can't lie, I want us to get to where we were. I want us to move forward. As a married couple." She places her hand on my arm and her eyes glisten. "But if you don't think you can get there, then maybe it's better for both of us if we step away from one another."

My chest tightens at the idea of her leaving again. "I told you I'd help you."

"But it's killing you. You think I don't see that? The tortured look on your face, the pain in your eyes. One minute we'll be having fun and it's like no time has passed, and the next you turn cold because you remember what I did."

"It's not because of what you did." I stand, unable to sit if she wants to have this conversation.

"Then what is it?" She stands but doesn't follow me.

I turn back to her. "You killed me! You crushed me! You wanna know what I did while you were away? I sat depressed by myself unless I was at work. I was miserable, a shell of my former self. I was stuck in the what-ifs and what-did-I-dos, trying to figure out how you could just leave me like that. I almost fell off the fucking mountain I was climbing because I was distracted and had no sleep. That was my wake-up call that I had to do something to get you out of my head. And just when I was getting there, you come strolling back into town with no memory of destroying us."

"I'm sorry." She sniffles and I can tell she's trying her best not to cry.

I clench my fists at my sides. "Stop saying you're fucking sorry!"

"Well I am!" she yells back. "I want to find out so maybe we can move on from it. I want to scream at the old me and say 'how could you have done this to the man you love.' I'm angry too, but do you know how hard it is for me to live with knowing I was the one who ruined us? Knowing that if we can't move forward, I'm the one to blame for my entire life imploding?"

We stare at each other, silent for a few moments. It feels good to have spoken the words out loud, but at the same time, it feels as though we've thrown a grenade and a crater is the only thing left between us.

"I'm not sure where that leaves us." I rub the back of my neck.

"I think we part. Maybe I should just go back to the inn and you can rent out the house. I'll sign the divorce papers like you wanted."

My heart aches with the thought of those damn papers.

"What?" she asks, stepping forward, all too familiar with my nonverbal expressions. "Talk to me, Adam. We were always good at talking. At least from what I remember."

"I feel like I'm stuck on a tightrope a hundred feet up in the air with a lion on one end and an alligator on the other. There's no escaping the pain, I just have to decide if I want to die by being shredded alive or swallowed whole. Because the thought of putting my heart out there again is just as excruciating as letting you slip out of my grasp again."

She places her hand on my chest and steps closer until I smell the scent of her shampoo. "I'm scared too. What if I'm not the girl you fell in love with? I know I'm different. I see it in people's expressions when I don't do what they expect me to. Maybe I'm not the Lucy you love anymore."

"What if your memory comes back and you decide I'm

not what you want? That we did marry too young and you want to leave and go live your life?"

"Or what if you can't stand my annoying new traits or are unable to deal with the fact I won't ever remember everything? There're a million what-ifs. I wish there wasn't, but we can't ignore them."

I cover her hand with mine. "It was so easy the first time around."

"Maybe that's the problem." She looks at me, searching my face with her big blue eyes. "I'm all in if you are. I'll put my fears aside because you're that important to me. But I understand if you can't. There'll be no hard feelings and I'll sign the papers. But I'm struggling with this middle road we've found ourselves on. I just need to know."

She rises up on her tiptoes and kisses my cheek, pausing with her lips there for a moment, then turns back toward the blanket. I grab her wrist before her hand slips off my chest.

She stops but doesn't turn around. "Please, only if you honestly mean it." The hiccup in her voice tells me she's about to cry.

I tug her toward me, and my hand cradles her cheek, my thumb brushing a tear away. "I want to fight for us."

"What are you saying?" she asks, her eyes heavy with love and lust.

"I'm in. You've always been mine, Lucy Greene. I've fought for you my entire life and I'm not giving up on us yet."

Her hand covers mine and she squeezes. Then I get to do what I've wanted to since she returned. I bend my neck and place my lips on hers.

Home at fucking last.

Chapter Twenty-two

"I'm perfect."

~Lucy Greene

Lucy

I've kissed Adam in many stages of his life. I've had his lips as a tentative adolescent, a horny teenage boy, a hesitant virgin, then a sexy man. But this kiss feels new. The slow lick of his tongue along the seam of my lips ignites a shiver down my spine. The groan that rumbles from his throat when I open my mouth strums a beat of thirst between my legs. His tongue strokes mine and I'm lost, feeling as if I'm his favorite dessert and he's savoring me moment by moment.

I wrap an arm around his neck and press my other hand against his chest. I can't tell whose heartbeat is faster, his or mine. This kiss is everything I've dreamed about since I returned, and my fingers fist his shirt so he doesn't try to pull away. We've been through too much, it's taken us too long to get here to stop now.

He tears his lips from mine and I groan, but his head falls into the crook of my neck, kissing every inch of my skin as if he's afraid he'll miss a spot. "God, you're fucking delicious."

"Don't stop. Please don't stop," I beg. My eyes close and my head tilts in whatever direction he dictates. I'm a slave to his touch and his kisses.

"Never. I can't believe I've lasted this long." He pulls back, his hazel eyes smoldering. Please tell me he isn't having second thoughts. "Only we would choose the middle of nowhere to start this."

I jump up and he catches me. "I don't care, just take me."

"Here?" He looks around.

There isn't anyone around for miles, which is the great thing about Alaska. "Yes."

He grabs my ass and walks me over to the four-wheeler to grab another blanket, then he walks us over to the one already set on the ground. "You've always had me tied around your finger."

"Don't act like you wanted to go back on that four-wheeler and wait until we get home."

"I never said that. It's just you were never a—"

I wrap my hand around the back of his neck and pull him down to me. I don't want to talk about what the old Lucy liked and didn't. I want to discover what I like with him now.

We lie down and our hands fiddle with each other's clothing. I go for the button and zipper on his jeans. He opens my vest and pushes my shirt up and over my head, leaving me in a pale blue bra.

He stares at me for a moment. "Fucking hell, you ruin me every damn time. I'm going to feast on your tits." His body falls over mine on the blanket, his lips grazing my neck right below my ear. His breath grows heavier in my ear as he grinds his bulge into my core. "We have way too many barriers on."

He gets up on his knees, unbuttoning my pants and tugging them down my body, but then we realize my boots need to come off first.

"Worst fucking clothes for this," he mumbles.

He's cute when he's flustered and even sexier because he can't wait to get me naked. I help him by standing, taking off my boots, and shimmying out of my jeans.

"Wait." He puts up his hand to stop me before I sit back down. "I wish I could snap a picture."

He reaches behind his head and pulls off his T-shirt, and I'm rewarded with the sight of his hard, muscular chest. Dropping to my knees, I slide my hand down the ridges of his abs, dipping under the elastic waistband of his boxer briefs. His hard, long length weighs heavy in my hands, and he inhales a deep breath and closes his eyes.

Again I'm reminded of all the stages of Adam I've been with. The first time I touched his dick, he almost came immediately. I laugh as I remember and ruin the moment between us.

"Why are you laughing while touching my dick?" Even with his question, he's reaching behind my back and unclasping my bra.

"I was thinking about the first time I touched you."

"Seriously? Right now you're having a memory?" He groans, sliding the straps of my bra down my shoulders.

"I can't control it."

"You could've pretended not to remember when I was a three-pump chump." His gaze dips to my breasts and he sighs, licking his lips. "I'm remembering the first time I sucked on those. Prepare yourself because I'm going to make up for lost time."

He gets me on my back, my hand having no choice but to let go of him.

"Get naked first." I push at his chest. "I want to feel us together."

"Bossy girl."

He kisses me one last time, then stands and unties his boots, hops on one leg to get the first one off, then the next. By the time his pants are off, my mouth is watering at the look of him. He's so... manly. So big everywhere. So muscled. Since the last time I remember being with him was when I was nineteen, it's like he's a different person. A very grown-up Adam.

"I think she likes what she sees." He waggles his eyebrows.

"You'd be right." I crook my finger and he lies down on top of me, pulling the other blanket over us.

It's not exactly sunbathing weather out here. Our bare legs slide along one another's while our naked flesh presses together.

"God, you're so hard," I say, not just talking about the bulge pressing against my clit, but his entire body.

"You're so soft." His hand runs down my arm and under my ass while grinding against me.

But my pussy needs more. It needs him to fill it, so I widen my legs, hoping he gets the hint that I'm barely hanging on here.

He chuckles and slides down my body, his mouth taking my right breast. Sucking and licking, making good on his promise that he'd spend a good amount of time there. He toys with my nipples, flicking with his tongue, then blowing a light stream of air. My back arches off the ground.

"I don't need foreplay," I say, my fingers diving into his hair.

I prop up on my elbows and he looks up at me through those dark eyelashes, a devilish grin in place. "Yeah, we're not rushing this."

My head falls back as he kisses down my stomach, nestling between my legs. He masterfully gets my panties off, situating himself so one of my legs is over his shoulder. I'm not going to be able to hold back.

"I should remind you that I haven't had an orgasm by anyone other than myself in a really long time."

He doesn't respond but runs two fingers through my folds before he laps at me. I jolt, my hips unable to control themselves, greedy and begging for more of his attention right where I need it the most.

"Oh god, Adam."

He blows another hot stream of air over me and shivers run up my spine. As he continues to lick and suck me, I have no control over the noises leaving me. Praises, curses, moans. Nothing has ever felt this fantastic.

"Don't stop. Ever."

He releases one hand off my hip then pushes a finger inside me, making my ass catapult off the ground. A deep chuckle vibrates against my pussy, but he doesn't relent. I grind my clit on his tongue as though I'm starting a fire with two sticks.

And then it comes, that little spark that grows bigger and hotter. I ride it all the way until I'm clenching and crying out, coming so hard I'm way too sensitive for him to continue. I close my legs because all my nerve endings are raw and satisfied now.

He looks up at me through my legs, rising on his knees, and brings his fingers to his mouth, licking them clean. "Just as good as I remember."

I laugh as he falls over me.

"I have bad news," he whispers then kisses me. The taste of me on him satisfies a primal need inside me, as though it's proof that he's mine.

"What?" I lock my legs around his waist.

"I don't have a condom with me. I wasn't thinking this would happen today."

I stare at him. "What if I told you I have an IUD?"

"I'd probably wonder why, but I'd be happy as fuck right now." He props up on his elbows and my fingernails scrape along his scalp.

"You know how I'd been on the pill? After the accident, my mom and I decided on an IUD so I wouldn't have to remember when to take the pill. That's all. It's not because I was sexually active with anyone."

He smooths my hair away from my forehead, and I prepare myself for him to say he doesn't know if he's clean. That me breaking him took him down a road of sleeping with numerous women. At the very least he must've slept with Alicia.

I hate myself again for ever leaving him and putting us in this awkward situation.

"I haven't slept with anyone since you," he says, his eyes locked with mine. "You might not believe me, but I just couldn't."

"Alicia?"

He shakes his head. "We never got there. I told you, you destroyed me. I didn't want anyone. I just wanted you."

We stay there, gazes fixed on one another's. How can I be lucky enough to get this guy twice in my lifetime? I must have a kick-ass fairy godmother somewhere.

"Then take me, Adam."

As though the words are exactly what he was hoping to hear, he pulls down the waistband of his boxer briefs. I help him, and once they're off, he situates himself between my legs, the tip of his dick right at my opening.

"You sure about this?" he asks.

"Yes."

He inches in the smallest bit. "Are you okay?"

"I'm not a virgin, remember? You were there."

A million-dollar smile lands on his face and he thrusts into me so deep and so fast, I gasp.

He grinds into me, circles, and does this thing with his hips that drives the desire right to the forefront, begging to be released. But I clench down, not even close to wanting this to end. I grab his shoulder blades, my nipples scraping along his chest every time he thrusts, sweat beading along his hairline. The blanket slips down to my feet, but my body is heated anyway.

He drives in and out of me, building my climax until I won't be able to hang on much longer.

"I can't. I'm going to," I pant, tightening my thighs and arching my back, my body screaming for the release.

"There's more to come, let it go," he says.

Every muscle in my body tenses, my orgasm ripping through my shaking body.

"Fuucck," he growls.

He fucks me hard and fast without abandon until he gasps and rocks inside me one final time before his body tightens above me and he growls. Once he's spent himself inside me, he lowers down on top of me, not giving me all his weight. I close my eyes and tilt my head to the side, exhausted even from being on the bottom.

He places his finger on my cheek and forces me to look at him. "You okay?"

I smile and lean up to kiss him, full of joy. "I'm perfect."

"Me too." He falls to my side and we lie facing the sun, completely naked.

Although I didn't want to talk about my memories or anything that came with them today, this is the most progress we've made so far. Adam's resilience amazes me. If only what had happened could disappear, I might finally feel at peace.

"Then I better do an A-plus job."
-Lucy Greene

Adam

After we get the four-wheeler back on the trailer, we stop and pick up wings and beer at Truth or Dare Brewery. Since we agreed we didn't want to be stuck there, I ran in and picked up the order to go.

"I'm tempted to ask what I used to like, but I'm not going to." Lucy bites into a buffalo-style wing and immediately pants like a dog, waving her hand.

"Want some milk?" I ask.

She shakes her head and sips her beer. "I'm good. But if I did like buffalo then, more power to the old Lucy."

I laugh and hold out one of my honey barbeque wings. "Want to try mine?"

She nuzzles closer and her thigh lands against mine. We opted to change into our pajamas and veg in front of the television when we got home, which turned into a quickie on the stairs before we came up for air. I've been drooling over her tits in that threadbare T-shirt for weeks. A starved man can only hang on so long when there's a juicy steak in front of him.

She leans forward and takes a bite of my wing. She looks up in the air and her head tilts right and left as though she's a professional judge. "I like that one. Sweet but with a tang."

I shake my head and hand her my box of wings, grabbing my beer from the table.

"No, they're yours," she says.

"Have them. I'm good with the medium ones too. Plus I ordered one of their quesadillas."

"That does look good." She stares at it while I pull out a triangle. The cheese pulls as though it doesn't want to part with the remaining portion of the meal.

"Have some. It's their specialty."

"I'm not gonna keep stealing your food." She hands me back the wings and studies the other wing flavors we grabbed.

Molly asked why I had so many flavors and I lied, telling her Cora and Toby were trying them out on Brody. She looked confused, but what does she know about kids anyway?

"This is *our* food." I run my hands over the table. "Not mine or yours. *Ours.*"

"Still, you ordered that for yourself."

I lean back on the couch, stretching my arm out along the back, facing her. "I have a request before we continue?"

She raises an eyebrow. "Okay."

"I can't handle any secrets. I promise to be an open book, but you have to promise the same, okay?"

"Yeah, of course." She nods.

"Then tell me why you're making a big deal about my wings and quesadillas?"

She sips her beer and stares at the wing selection again.

I lean forward, placing my finger under her chin and turning her face to mine. "What's up, Lucy?"

Her teeth bite into her bottom lip and she shrugs. "I have this feeling that I used to get my way all the time. That I steamrolled you into doing what I wanted."

A laugh leaves me, and I bend forward, shaking my head. "That's every relationship. Do you think I was some doormat who let you dictate all my moves? That I starved myself so you got what you wanted?"

"More or less, yeah?" Her eyes don't reach mine.

"I hate to break this to you, but if Nikki was next to me right now and she wanted my wings, I'd probably offer them to her too. That's not specific to you, although I'd give you a lot more than I would my stepsister. It's just me. It's who I am. Who most men are with the women they love. I've been racking my brain for a way to show you that I didn't sacrifice anything by being with you. I was exactly where I wanted to be."

"Are you sure though?" She peeks up at me with the piercing blue eyes that drew me to her as soon as my hormones went crazy and noticed girls.

"I'm positive. Would I have been devastated when you left if you were such a horrible person? I don't think so."

She snuggles up to me and lays her head on my shoulder, her finger running over the words on my T-shirt. "I'm terrified you're in love with someone who doesn't exist anymore, but at the same time, I'm afraid I was a crappy wife you put on an undeserved pedestal."

"Damn, you need to turn your brain off." I nudge her to get up and direct her hips to straddle me. I place my hand on her cheeks. "We decided to throw all that shit out the window. I love this new Lucy thing you're trying out, but that doesn't change how I feel about the old Lucy either.

She's still here, you know?" I place a hand over her heart. "You can't erase her, and I don't want you to."

She leans forward, her tits pressing to my chest. "Okay," she says unconvincingly.

"Say it with more gusto."

"Okay," she says a little louder, and I allow her the reprieve so we can have an enjoyable night.

"There you go." I place my lips on hers. I'm never going to grow tired of kissing her now that I know what it's like not to be able to. "You still have two more to try. The two hottest ones."

She shakes her head. "No way. I won't have any taste buds left."

"Do you wanna know which one you loved?"

"I'm guessing honey barbeque?"

I shake my head. "Inferno."

"Really?" Her eyes widen.

I shake my head and chuckle.

"What then?"

"You didn't eat wings."

Her forehead falls to my shoulder. "I think I'm getting farther away from the old me rather than closer."

I wrap my arms around her and kiss her temple. "You're just more open to new things now. Nothing wrong with that."

She nestles into my neck. "Adam?"

My hand runs down the hair splayed against her back. "Yeah?"

"Will you sleep with me tonight?"

I stiffen for a moment. I'm not sure I can go into our old bedroom just yet. Especially with all the boxes of our old life filling the space. "How about you sleep with me tonight?"

She picks up her head to look at me.

"I'm not ready."

She stares for a moment before nodding. "Okay."

Eventually I'll need to address what that room represents, but for the moment, I'm going to enjoy getting this far.

I'M IN THE KITCHEN, packing my lunch for work, when Lucy walks down the stairs from the bedroom. It's been a few days, and although I'd rather be here with her, I have to go to work. We've been hiding out since we don't want our business everywhere, but it's time for me to get back to my regular routine. Plus, she wants to tell her mom today, which should go as well as putting a cheetah and an antelope in the same cage.

I pour her coffee and slide it across the counter. She doesn't pick it up but instead comes right over to me. She switched up her pajamas last night, wearing a tank top and shorts, saying she's warmer in bed with me than when she's alone.

"Good morning," I say before kissing her.

She wraps her arms around my waist. "I was going to wake you up with a blow job this morning, but you wore me out last night."

We've been going at one another like fucking bunnies. Thank god she has an IUD, otherwise I would've made a condom run at least three times by now and it probably would've ended up on Nikki's show. I haven't walked around with a hard-on this much since I was fourteen.

"And what brought on this plan?"

"Wanted to make sure you were thinking of me today," she says, her fingers inching down my stomach.

"No worries, I'll be thinking about what I'm gonna do to you when I get home."

She takes one of my hands and slides it up her chest. The brash movement makes my dick twitch.

"Oh, I got a reaction," she says, obviously feeling it since her other hand is right by my crotch. She slides her tongue out of her mouth, gives me her seductive glare, and shakes her hips before falling to her knees in front of me.

"I can't be late," I say like an idiot.

She takes the strap of my utility belt, sliding it out and unhooking it. "Then I better do an A-plus job."

I step back to lean on the counter, knowing I'm going to need the support.

In no time flat, my pants are open and pushed down to pool at my ankles. She pulls down my boxer briefs, and my dick pops up between us like a jack-in-the-box.

She moves forward, her tongue running up the length of my cock, staring at me for a reaction the entire time. Then her fingers wrap around my base and my cock jumps in excitement that it gets to start its morning like this.

My fingers thread through her dark strands, not about to miss a second of her lips on me. She brings the leaking tip of my cock to her lips, sweeping her tongue across it while her fist pumps me, and my dick aches for more. She wraps her entire mouth over my dick, taking me all the way to the back of her throat. The strands of her hair tighten in my hand from the lurch of my body coming off the counter.

Damn, her mouth is still fucking amazing.

She works me expertly with the precision of someone who knows her way around a dick, my dick, doing everything I love. She might not remember all the things from her past, but she remembers exactly what gets me off during a blow job.

"Fuck," I say, unable to stop myself from thrusting into her mouth.

She moans, licking up my underside. Fuck, I'm gonna nut in her mouth right now. The noises she's making in the quiet of our home are driving me crazy.

I put my hands on the counter, wanting to give her the control to take me wherever she wants. For her to feel the power she has over me, that I'm hers and only hers, forever.

That seems to spur her enjoyment, and she torments me with her mouth and her hand simultaneously. She's not looking up at me and waiting for me to come, but it's like she's enjoying her mouth on me. When she reaches her hand under the waistband of her shorts, I'm done.

"I'm gonna come," I groan.

She doesn't stop and I moan as I come in her mouth. She swallows and licks my now sensitive tip.

Fuck, how I missed this.

"Now you can go to work." She pulls up my boxer briefs and my pants, sliding me back inside, then buckles my utility belt.

"I think I'm coming down with something." I put the back of my hand on my forehead.

She laughs and rises to her tiptoes. She kisses me, and tasting myself on her tongue is fucking glorious. Jesus, I want to spend the day here with her. I take a quick glance at the clock. Yeah, I'm gonna be late.

I grab her hips and hoist her on the counter, then tear off her pajama shorts and push her shirt up to see her tits.

"You have work," she says.

"They'll deal. If I don't taste you this morning, I'll be distracted all day."

I nestle between her legs and get her off quicker than

ever. Who said mornings suck? Today is a goddamn beautiful day.

Chapter Twenty-four

Lucy

I go out on the deck to call my mom, hoping that the beautiful scenery will keep me in a serenity state when I tell her I've reignited the flame with Adam. Although I'm not keen on everyone in town knowing about us, one thing is certain—it won't stay only our business for long. If my mom hears it from someone else, her wrath will be worse.

She answers on the third ring, which tells me she's probably busy. The woman usually answers my phone calls in one ring, sometimes half a ring, because she's so worried about me.

"Lucy?" she answers as though she thinks someone else would be calling from my phone.

"Hey, Mom," I say.

"How are you? Anything else come back?"

I'm quiet for a moment, knowing I need to find that old part of myself that was strong enough to walk away from my family because of their disapproval. Although I'm hoping this time is different. That we can figure this out.

"Well, I remember my wedding," I say.

"That's good." She says it as if I just said I went on a walk. No inflection in her tone.

"Yeah, and I have some other news."

"Oh?"

She's pretending to be bored with the conversation. As though she doesn't want to hear from me. I have to think she's acting the same way she did then. Her indifference to what's going on makes me angry.

"I'm seeing Adam again."

Dead silence.

"Mom?"

"I'm here," she says.

I blow out a breath and look at the trees and the mountains, wishing for some peace. "We've decided that we're going to move forward even though my memory hasn't returned."

"Hmm."

"Mom, please say something else." I roll my eyes because she's acting like a child.

It takes her a minute to speak. "And what happens when your memory does come back and you realize why you left him? What are you going to do? Run away again?"

"No." I shake my head although she can't see me. "I'm going to stay here. Whatever the reason was, it doesn't matter anymore. We've agreed to be truthful with one another. Whatever it is, we'll work through it."

"How do you know the reason won't still be an issue for you?"

I open my mouth and stop for a second. "You sound like you know what the reason is."

She guffaws. "How would I know, Luce? You told me nothing. I'm just saying it could still come back and be an issue for you both. You're both playing with your hearts if you think this is some love story gone wrong. You act like you're naive as to how hard it is to love someone, like Cupid came and shot arrows in you, like nothing bad can happen." Her voice grows louder.

"We love one another, yes. But we're not naive. We know how hard we'll have to work on this."

"Jesus, Lucy," she says.

There's a long beat of deafening silence. I wait it out, denying the part of me that wants to fill it with something. But at this point, my words would only be mean-spirited and I want things to be different this time around.

"Fine. Good luck then. I hope it works out."

"Doesn't sound like you actually feel that way."

"What do you want me to say? This is why I didn't want you in that town. They swallow you up and before you know it, you're drinking the Greene family Kool-Aid!" she yells.

A bunch of birds fly out of a tree near me. I wish I could fly away with them.

"They love me. Which brings up another question. Did I leave a necklace there?" I touch my bare neck. I still haven't found that necklace, but I'm sure it has to be somewhere.

"A necklace? No."

"And not my journal either?" There's no way I would've destroyed them. I know that deep down to my bones. I could've never done that to Adam. Destroy something of his mother's.

"No, Lucy, you kept that part of your life hidden from us. I guess we were okay for you to run to when it all went bad, but now you're going to pretend you don't have a family again."

The phone creaks as I clench it. "You're the one doing it to me. You're the one who didn't come to my wedding."

"I don't agree with you marrying into that family. There was a reason you came home, Lucy. I want you to think about that. You're turning a blind eye to why you walked out on your marriage, but you must've felt you couldn't be there anymore. Someone must've said or done something."

"Mom," I sigh. "What don't you understand? The Greenes are good people. Ignore all the bullshit from the feud between the two sides of the family. What have they ever done to make you hate them so much?"

I'm met with another bout of silence. I roll my eyes. "I—"

"Lucy," my dad comes on the phone. "You know your mom's feelings on this issue. Nothing is going to change."

"Well, maybe it should. Maybe you should get to know people before you judge them off of someone else's experience with them."

"Don't sass me," my dad warns. "Your mom has slaved over you for the last three months and what have you done? You turn your back to go to those people after she almost lost her job caring for you."

I swallow down the guilt that anyone had to sacrifice anything because of my accident. "I'm sorry for that, but I love Adam. He's my husband and that's that."

"And here we go again. It's like déjà vu," my mom comes back on the line.

"Then I guess we'll just go back to not being in each other's lives."

I click End and cock my arm back to throw my phone deep into the woods, but my fingers clench around it and I bring it down, releasing a scream that echoes through the forest. I release a breath and close my eyes. Time to channel this energy into something good. My parents have no idea what they're talking about. But they sure know how to plant a seed of doubt because now I'm wondering—what if history repeats itself?

I shake my head. No. I know in my bones this is where I belong.

IN THE AFTERNOON, I call an Uber to take me into downtown Sunrise Bay. Eventually I'll have to get a car, because getting my SUV from my parents is probably not an option at this point. Not to mention, I want to start fresh. If Adam saw me drive away in that SUV, I don't want him thinking about it every time he sees it.

The Uber drops me off in the town square and I set my eyes on The Grind. I've been meaning to come by and see Zoe since I remembered her last week. Adam had been drinking a coffee and her and her shop came back to me. I'm here to try some different coffees.

"Lucy!" she calls when I walk in, abandoning the customer she's with and running around the counter to give me a big hug.

"Hey, Zoe," I say, hugging her back.

How can my parents not love this town?

She draws back, her hands on my upper arms. "I should put you over my knee for waiting so long to come in."

"Sorry. Believe it or not, I've been busy, and I don't have a car, so I'm at the mercy of others."

"Well, you're here now. Let me get you your—"

"Wait," I rush out before she says my usual order. I think Adam's starting to think I'm crazy for testing all these new foods and drinks, but it gives me a sense of control I haven't felt since my accident. "Can I try a few different things? I'm doing this thing where I try to figure out what I like now, not back before I lost my memory."

She smiles and winks. "You got it. Have a seat and I'll bring some out to you."

I walk over to the counter, her employee helping the poor man Zoe left. "I'd rather talk to you while you make them, if you don't mind."

"Mind? Not at all." She gets busy using machines I can't imagine I'd ever figure out. "So what's new?"

"Um... nothing." I bite down my smile with the hopes that she doesn't suspect anything.

"Don't give me that. How's Adam? Are you guys figuring things out?"

"Well, I'm figuring out that I was a tad selfish in our rela-tionship."

She frowns and sighs. "Who said that? Men are supposed to kiss the feet of their wives. Why do you think there's that saying, 'happy wife, happy life'?"

The fact she doesn't refute my previous personality makes me think I'm right. I'd love to ask someone if people in this town thought I wasn't deserving of Adam, but at this point, everyone's coddling me.

"How are things here?" I look around at the almost full house and smile.

Zoe partnered with Adam's mom to start The Grind back when Mrs. Greene first started her family, but now it's just Zoe's.

"Really good. I have a muffin lady." She nods toward a case in the front. "Pick one. They're so good."

"A muffin lady?" I say, looking them over.

"Yep, one day she's going to become famous and leave me." She leans forward. "They are that delicious, I swear."

She goes back to making coffee. "But for now, I have a muffin lady."

I giggle at her exuberant behavior. I never knew Adam's mother well. I'd see her at school and things, and she was really friendly, always smiling. I have to think if she had a friend like Zoe, then she must've been just as fun-loving.

The phone rings and Zoe glances at her employee who's still explaining the difference between espresso and coffee.

"Now go sit and relax. I'll be right there." Zoe walks over and answers the phone. "The Grind."

I find a table in the back that looks across at Truth or Dare Brewery and The Story Shop. The big sign of Cade Greene's public announcement to Presley Knight is still up between the two places. They make a cute couple. I'm glad Cade found the one for him.

I ignore a few people's lingering looks. Some smile and carry on with their conversations. Others don't. Checking to see how Zoe is doing with my coffees, I see that she's on the phone still. She shoots me a wave, and when I rise to get the coffees, she shoos me back down with her hand.

A minute later, she walks over with five small drinks. "Here you go. I figured we'd start basic. You've got cappuccino, latte, mocha, americano, and black. I'm curious which you'll pick, so you let me know which one the new Lucy enjoys. Although..." She places her hand on mine. "The old Lucy was pretty magnificent too."

"Thanks, Zoe." I lean over and smell all the coffees. Delicious.

Picking up the black, I inhale the scent and tip the cup to my lips. Just like Adam makes at home. I wonder if there's a family recipe I don't know about.

Then I continue around the circle of coffees, trying some twice, others three or even four times. I'm not sure I even want to pick one. They're all wonderful, but my fave of faves is the cappuccino.

Zoe comes by now that a rush is over. "Want a muffin from my lady?"

I shake my head. "No, but I think I'd like a cappuccino?"

"Sure thing." She starts to walk away but stops, watching someone through the window. Then the door of The Grind opens. "Oh, hang on to your hat, here comes trouble," she mumbles.

Grandma Ethel and Dori walk into the small cafe, their eyes set on me. Isn't one wild, heart-stopping drive with them enough for one person's lifetime?

Chapter Twenty-five

Adam

I lie on the couch after a long day of work. "I can't believe you let my grandma suck you in."

"She cornered me. I guess it's something I used to plan for them." Lucy lies on me and kisses me. "And you used to come with me apparently."

It's unreal how much I took this for granted at one time. "I don't want to spend our night entertaining old people drawing weird things. Plus, they argue all the time and it's annoying."

"What can I do to persuade you?" She wiggles on me, her core sliding along my crotch.

"Keep doing that and we're not going anywhere." I still her hips with my hands.

"How about a little strip tease afterward?" She sits up and grabs the hem of her shirt, pulling it up her torso.

"No sense if we can't finish. Let's just get this over with." I groan and move her off my lap so I can go take a shower. "I swear they're the only retirement center up past six." I head up the stairs to the bathroom, but I stop at the top and look at her below. "Did you talk to your mom today?"

Lucy's smile dims. "I did."

I lean on the railing at the top of the stairs. "I take it things didn't go well?"

She pulls her knees up to her chest. "You take it right."

I mentally curse Susan. I want to tell Lucy how much better off she is without them. But instead, I inhale a deep breath. "Well, maybe we just keep trying. If it's important to you."

"They're pretty set in their decision."

"Well, they were set in it before, but they welcomed you with open arms after you left Sunrise Bay."

She stands, and my eyes follow her across the room to the stairs. She starts to climb them.

Grandma Ethel better give me the best grandson award after this. Look what I'm missing out on by leaving tonight.

"I didn't go home to them right away," she says. "My mom said I wasn't home long before I fell off the horse. Where would I have gone?"

"I wish I knew."

She meets me at the top of the stairs. "Me too."

My hands land on her hips and she steps forward until we're chest to chest.

"We can be a little late." She strips off her shirt, tossing it on the floor.

I'll let her distract herself this once, but sooner or later, we're going to have to figure this out. Her parents are going to be the same issue they were when we first got together.

AN HOUR LATER, I park my truck outside Northern Lights Retirement Center. Lucy started twice-monthly drawing nights years ago when Grandma Ethel acted as though the peeps at Northern Lights Retirement Center were twiddling their thumbs in boredom. It was nice of Lucy, and even though I don't want to be here, how could I argue with her? I know her agenda is to get me to spend quality time with my grandma.

Lucy puts her arm through mine. "Relax, it's only an hour. Didn't you enjoy it before?"

I only enjoy when I'm left alone to draw, which doesn't happen here—ever. I shrug in answer to her question. "So are we telling my grandma we're a couple again? Because if we do, she's gonna tell everyone."

She stops right before we get to the entrance. "It's up to you. What do you want to do?"

I'm not really up for a secret relationship, but I'm also not up for public humiliation if this blows up in my face. I hate the idea of a town scandal and gossip about the two of us.

"What are you comfortable with?" I run my finger along her hairline and tuck the one strand that's fallen out of her ponytail behind her ear.

"Whatever you're comfortable doing."

"I'd like us to come out. Better than people catching wind of it and making up their own narrative."

She smiles and presses her body to mine. "I guess we're coming out."

"Only if you want."

"I always loved being your girl, Adam." She kisses me one more time and walks inside, turning around right as the doors slide open. "Come on. They don't bite."

I shake my head and follow her. Hell, I'd follow her off a cliff, that's how much I love this woman.

It only takes five minutes in the drawing room for me to regret my decision to follow Lucy.

"She's more beautiful, don't you think?" Dori says from next to me. I got stuck between her and Earl. "More confident. Sure of herself."

I nod, sitting at my easel.

"She was always good at organizing these things." Grandma leans over Dori as though she's whispering, but she's really talking as loudly as she always does, interrupting the instructor Lucy scored last minute.

Lucy is a teacher but wasn't an art major, so they bring in an expert to teach the class on how to draw or paint on canvas. I usually just do my own thing. I'd be game if I got to sit next to Lucy during these art nights, but she passes out the materials and makes sure everyone is doing okay while the instructor at the front of the class leads everyone step by step. That leaves me with these two elderly women who think they're Thelma and Louise or something. I'm not joking, they actually call themselves that.

"I told you we're together. Why you still playing matchmaker?" I ask Grandma, who shakes her head at me. "I heard about Cade and Presley's game night here, Grandma. You're not fooling anyone, you know that, right?"

She rolls her eyes and turns her attention up front.

"Okay, everyone," the instructor, Leslie, says between the easels that are set up in a circle around her own. Leslie explains how we're going to sketch out the drawing first, then we'll go into the painting and that Lucy will be around if anyone needs more paint or a different paintbrush.

"Do you think she's going to model naked?" Earl asks me.

"No."

"Man." He puts his pencil back in the holder. "They trick me every time. It's the only reason I come." He shakes his head and crosses his arms like the kids from Lucy's class.

Fun night. I should make sure Lucy plans another.

"Earl!" Grandma points at him. "You said you were going to participate."

"Yeah," Dori chimes in. "You took a spot from someone else."

He rolls his eyes at me and picks up his pencil again.

Leslie talks about the progression of the trees going from smaller to larger.

"Progression? Hell, all I see is regression these days. My damn dick is shrinking by the minute." Earl nods at me when I stare at him in disbelief.

My gaze falls to my lap as though he's got to be talking smack.

"Just wait until your balls drop to your ankles." He elbows me.

"You sure there's no alcohol allowed tonight?" I scour the area.

"No, remember when Martha fell over and broke her hip? Now we all have to suffer because of her 'little problem.'" Dori uses air quotes.

If we do this again, I'm smuggling in a flask.

"Poor Martha," I say.

"She walks three miles a day now. That new hip gave her new life," Dori says.

"And rehab," Earl leans over and whispers in my ear.

"How's everyone doing?" Lucy comes by, putting her hand on my shoulder and kissing my cheek.

When she stands straight, Dori and Grandma have hearts in their eyes. Okay, I might too.

"I'd like you to find me some alcohol, and Earl would like to lodge a complaint that the instructor isn't stripping," I say.

"Earl!" Dori scolds.

"I'm a man. I haven't seen real live titties in years."

My body shivers—and not in a good way.

Lucy puts her hand on his shoulder and leans in close. "Let's use our inside voices. We don't want to scare our guest."

"Sorry, Lucy," Earl says. "Sometimes those two are so judgmental."

"I hear ya," I say.

Lucy squeezes my shoulder before continuing around the room. For a moment, I'm able to push all the noise around me somewhere else and zone in on my drawing. But I don't draw mountains or trees or a sunset with glistening snow. Instead, I draw a woman—my woman. From memory. It's her smile that captivates me, and I use charcoal to shade in my work, not about to add a speck of paint.

They call for a break because the residents can't sit on the stools too long without their ankles swelling.

"You should put her in a bikini," Earl says.

"This is a PG class." I turn the picture around during break so no one can see it. Although I'm a little terrified that Earl is going to beat off to my wife tonight regardless of whether I put a bikini on her or not.

The staff set up some cookies, coffee, and tea. It's a thankless job and the residents all complain, asking for decaf and sugar-free options because otherwise they'll be up all night and their blood sugar will rise.

Dori distracts Lucy before I can get to her, and Grandma blocks me into a corner.

"I think it's great that you found some forgiveness for

Lucy. I found her at The Grind today, trying different coffees. What's with this old Lucy, new Lucy crap?" she whispers.

"She's just trying to find herself, that's all." I stuff my hands in my pockets.

She pats my cheek. "Well, I'm proud of you for stepping out of your own way. Your grandfather would be so proud of the man you've become."

"Thanks, Grandma. Hopefully I'm not the center of embarrassment again in Sunrise Bay."

She glances over her shoulder at Lucy. "Don't tell her—because there was nothing wrong with her before—but I like the new her. She holds her shoulders higher. She looks like she's in charge of her destiny now." She grabs my shirt sleeve and turns me toward the sweets table. She stacks some cookies in a napkin. "You take these home for you and Lucy."

"We don't need any cookies."

"Who doesn't love something sweet before bedtime? They'll just go to waste with all the diabetics around here." She puts them in my hands and nudges for me to hide them.

"Where do you expect me to put them?"

"In your pocket. Hurry, here comes Ivy and she's a stickler for the rules. No food is supposed to leave the premises. But my fees pay for these treats, so it shouldn't matter if I give them to my grandson."

"Um..." I put them behind my back.

Ivy smiles at me, checking over the station. "Are y'all having fun?"

"The best." Grandma smiles way too big to not be suspicious.

After Ivy walks away, I say, "I'm pretty sure Ivy saw that

I'm hiding something, and I don't think she'll care if I eat some cookies."

She waves me off with a smile. "They're different when the families aren't here."

"Okay, that's cryptic and scary. Maybe clarify that? You're safe here, right?"

"Oh yeah, they're nice. Plus, we're not feeble. Half of us have canes. We'd revolt if they weren't. Now I gotta smuggle these to Lucy before we start up again."

I watch Grandma walk over to Lucy as though she's doing a drug deal with stolen cookies. Dori actually turns around to act like the lookout. It's so comical I can't help but laugh. Lucy just puts them in her purse and says thank you.

Grandma has a point. Maybe that's what it is with Lucy —she's holding herself differently. Not that she lacked self-esteem before, but she's almost like, 'Take me as I am, and I don't care if you like it or not.'

I know I sure as hell like it.

Chapter Twenty-six

Lucy

e're midway through the second half of the drawing night when a lady with a name tag that says Mrs. Pierce drags me down into the vacant chair next to her.

"I've always thought it was adorable how you did this for him. I heard the gossip. You know Ethel's always playing her granddaughter's gossip news radio station here. You lost your memory?"

I nod, feeling weird discussing this with someone I don't know.

"Yeah, I wondered why these nights just stopped abruptly. It all makes sense now."

I tilt my head. "What makes sense?"

Mrs. Pierce's painting is almost an identical replica of the instructor's, except she's added little details like a glow around the moon and the flurries of snow aren't just dots.

"Are you an artist?" I ask.

She laughs. "Well, you really did lose your memory then."

I frown. "So I knew that?"

She laughs again and pushes up her dark glasses. "Yeah, you did. We talked all the time about…" She nods toward Adam.

"We did?"

She leans closer. "His love of drawing. That's why you started organizing these nights. To get him to draw. You don't remember that, huh?"

I try to make sense of what she's suggesting, but why would I organize art nights at the retirement home so that Adam could draw? If he wanted to draw, he could have done it at home. I didn't have to drag him here.

"Lucy dear, will you see me back to my room?" Mrs. Pierce announces loudly.

Adam's gaze finds mine from across the way. He starts to rise, but I wave to tell him to sit down.

"Just get Ivy to help you, Iris," Earl says. "The girl doesn't want to see all your fancy things."

Iris stands and grabs the cane from next to her. "Shut up, you old fool." She points her cane at him.

I bite my lip to stop from laughing, and Adam shakes his head across the room.

We leave the room as the complaints start about how their trees don't look like trees and someone's mountains have no peaks.

Mrs. Pierce walks with purpose, and we get to her room down the hall. Earl was right, fancy is an understatement for her room. You'd think she brought in a decorator. Everything looks elegant and expensive. But it's her walls that amaze me. Paintings and drawings and sculpted art, every piece more beautiful than the last.

"Sit down." She goes to her fridge.

The great thing about Northern Lights is that it enables the residents to have apartments of their own, but the residence keeps them busy with extracurriculars.

She returns with a bottle of wine and two glasses, all the while walking with her cane.

"Oh, I'm not sure if I should drink. They're probably expecting me back."

"Suit yourself." She pours herself a glass of wine and sits in an ugly recliner instead of her gorgeous couch. "This was my Erwin's." She pats the chair's arm in a loving way. "He passed three years ago now." She points around the room. "You see all this? He said I could do whatever I wanted, he just wanted his recliner. So now it's the only seat I sit in. He was right to dig it out of the trash all the times I tried to throw it out."

"I can see that."

She sips the wine and places the bottle closer to me than her—probably as an invitation if I change my mind. "Since it's really only you and me who know this, I figured we should get away from all those ears. They act like they can't hear, but believe me, they turn those hearing aids up when they think someone's got gossip." She eyes me and nods.

I lean in. "Okay, what do only we know?"

"You came to Northern Lights about four years ago and said you were Ethel's granddaughter by marriage. Anyone who gets us off their hands is a saint to the staff, so when you volunteered to host a drawing class twice a month, they took you up on the offer."

"But I did for a reason other than to just be nice?"

When Ethel and Dori cornered me at The Grind, I thought maybe old Lucy wasn't as bad as I thought. She volunteered at a retirement center, so how selfish could she really be? But maybe I was wrong.

Mrs. Pierce shakes her head and sips her wine, leaving me in suspense. I'm about to grab that glass out of her hand and down it so she can fill me in on what the hell is going on.

"It took about a year before you trusted me enough to tell me. Your beloved didn't come with you one night and that spurred our conversation. Sure, you'd compliment all my paintings, but we never really talked. Plus, Ethel and Dori can be possessive, you know? I want to say, 'Hey, you have, like, thirty grandchildren between the two of you, ever hear of sharing?'"

My shoulders scrunch. Mrs. Pierce must not have any family around here.

"Right now, Ethel's probably trying to figure out why you're not back yet." She glances at the door as though that's a real threat.

"Okay, so why did I plan these nights if not just to be nice?"

She stares at me long and hard. "You did them for him."

"Him?"

"Your beloved. Adam. You said he used to love to draw and it had slowly stopped once you got married. That you never wanted him to stop something he loved, and this was a way to make sure that twice a month, he did it, even if you had to drag him kicking and screaming."

I pour myself a glass of wine and guzzle it. "Seriously?"

"Uh huh." Mrs. Pierce pats my leg. "Oh, when I told my Erwin that, he put his hand on mine and said, 'Those two will make it.'"

I agree, that's what love is all about, wanting the other

person to be happy above all else. Loving them so much to allow them to have the things they want no matter the sacrifice you have to make for yourself. "Why didn't I just tell him that?"

I think of the pact I made with Adam that we'd be truthful with one another from this point forward. How could I not say to him, "Hey, you need to draw, so I'm setting this up?"

"Because you wanted him to love it and not feel obligated to do it. You were releasing his spirit, his talent. You know those of us in the creative world don't like strict timelines to do what we want when someone else dictates. It's a shame he never returned the phone call from my old partner."

I'm so lost in thought, I almost missed what she said. "What phone call?"

"We sent a few of his drawings to my old partner in LA. Man, that horse sure did a number on you, sweetie."

"And Adam never returned the call?"

She shakes her head. "No. He's talented. I mean, I'm far removed from that world now, but I like his stuff." She pours herself another glass of wine. "Now you need to go. I don't need to hear it from Ethel in the morning."

She nudges my feet with her cane, and I hop off the couch.

I walk around her glass coffee table and I'm about to leave, but instead, I walk over to her and hug her. "Thank you."

She pats my back. "You're welcome. Now go."

I walk out of her room feeling lighter. She has no idea the gift she just gave me. I close the door and take a moment to take in exactly what she said. Maybe the old Lucy wasn't so bad. She obviously loved Adam a helluva lot to endure two nights a month here. I push away from the door to walk down the hall and spot Adam standing there.

"I was just coming to find you," he says.

"Sorry. Is time up?" We meet in the middle of the hall and his hands land on my hips and he pins me to the wall.

"I've wanted to get you alone all night." His lips land on mine and he kisses me until I'm breathless. "That's just an appetizer until later tonight." He winks, takes my hand, and guides me toward the room. "What did Mrs. Pierce want?"

"Just to see her back." I hate the way the lie tastes, but I need to soak this in some more. Allow me to see how much drawing means to Adam.

"They love you," he says.

We go into the activity room and almost everyone is packing up, putting their paintbrushes in the sink and laying their artwork on the drying racks.

"I'm beat. Thanks, Lucy." Dori hugs me.

Earl throws his canvas in the trash. "Garbage. Call me when you get the naked woman."

I pick it up and put it on the drying rack. Every piece is art.

Ethel hugs us both. "Don't crush the cookies," she whispers.

After I say goodbye to the instructor, Adam is lingering over his own canvas. I walk over to him and he slides his arm behind my back.

"You ready?" he asks.

I nod.

"You don't remember, but this was kind of a special moment between us for years."

I look at him. "What was?"

"Well, I don't draw what everyone else does. I draw what I want, and you always asked me to surprise you."

"Oh, I can't wait," I say.

He flips around the canvas and I sink into his hold. He drew me with my hand on my cheek and my hair down, framing my face. But I have a love-drunk smile on my face.

"I love it," I say before kissing his cheek.

"Good. Then we'll take it home."

Home has never sounded so good coming from his mouth.

After we clean the brushes and I say goodbye to Ivy and the other helpers, we turn off the lights to the room and walk out of Northern Lights Retirement Center hand in hand.

"Do you ever regret not going to school for art?" I ask.

He sighs. "Don't go rethinking all my life choices again. I told you, I'm happy."

"But it's not too late, you know. You could still do it."

He opens the passenger side truck door and kisses my nose. "I like my job. I'm happy where I am."

He shuts the door, and when he slides into his seat, he puts the picture in the back seat.

"It's just a suggestion," I say.

He starts the truck. "I will say this. I haven't drawn a thing in over a year. That felt good tonight. But what came out when I put pencil to paper is the most important thing in my life right now, and that's you."

"But, Adam..."

He shakes his head, putting the truck in gear. "Don't overthink this. I was never meant to be an artist. It's just a hobby I enjoy."

Then he pulls out of the parking lot, and there seems to be a finality to the conversation I don't like. Is this why I set up the art nights behind his back? God, please tell me I didn't leave him so he'd go be an artist in LA and we lost an entire year for nothing?

As good as things are between us, I know I wouldn't have left without a good reason.

Chapter Twenty-seven

"Not just sleep. Clothes in the closet, toiletries
in the bathroom."
-Lucy Greene

Adam

It's been a month since Lucy and I decided to be together again, and things are going great. I've yet to sleep in the master bedroom and she hasn't pushed me, although I'll find her in there sometimes, reading her journals or staring at pictures of us. Not a lot of memories have surfaced since Marla ambushed Lucy at their house and she recalled our wedding. For the most part, I've made my peace with the fact that we may never find out what caused her to leave, but that's only because she's a different Lucy now. The same still, but different. More open.

We're at my brothers' brewery today and they're telling her how they're going to name a beer after her.

"It's going to be called Lucy Takes Flight. We'll give them five different kinds of beer in small glasses." Jed places the setup in front of Lucy.

She glances at me before saying to Jed, "You're going to name something after me?"

"You're an ass," I say, shaking my head.

His forehead wrinkles. "What the hell are you talking about?"

"The name?" I raise my eyebrows. "Lucy Takes Flight." He and Lucy still look at me confused. "Referencing how she skipped town..."

"Jesus it's called that because it's a flight of beer, you idiot." He shakes his head at me.

"Oh, sorry." Lucy's frowning at me and I feel like an ass for assuming the worst.

"Anyway, moving on," Jed says. "We had Mr. Sanders make wooden planks for the flights."

Her hand falls over her heart and she glances at me and back at my brothers. "That's so sweet!" She leans over and hugs them both.

"It's going to be the hit of the season," Jed says and points at the first glass. "So you have our Razzle Dazzle, Naked Digger, Melting Heart, Limp Donkey, and No Stout For You."

"I think this is just their way of not making a beer for the season," I say, crossing my arms.

"Well, we toyed with Minderaser but didn't think it would sell. When Lucy came in to figure out which beer she liked best, the lightbulb went off," Cade says.

"Technically Molly thought of it," Jed says.

Cade rolls his eyes. It feels like he wants to say more but doesn't. I'm not sure what that's about, but if Jed's messing around with Molly, heads are gonna roll and Nikki's gonna be the one holding the ax.

"I love it." Lucy picks up Melting Heart.

"That's ours. Mine and Presley's." Cade smiles.

"It is not. It's from the duo night," Jed says with a scowl.

"I made that beer for her, it's ours."

My brothers walk away, bickering about who the beer belongs to.

"They'll never stop fighting over who makes the best beer this place sells." I nod toward the Melting Heart in her hand. "That was their best seller last year."

"I love the apricot taste." After she sips it, I lean over to kiss her.

"So, I was thinking…" I begin the conversation I've started in my head a million times over. "We should probably talk about the future. Not that I want to pressure you."

She turns in her chair. Thankfully, we're at a corner table away from the other customers, who are mostly tourists anyway. "What about the future?"

"Well, we're living together. You still have my name. Next week is technically two months since we made our agreement." Man, that day at the inn when she refused to sign the divorce papers seems so long ago. We've come so far from that moment. "I think we need to move on as though your memory isn't going to return."

She twists the glass in the holder. "And if it does?"

"Then we deal with it. We're different, right? We'll talk it out and go from there. But I want us to start building our life together again."

"Like kids?" Her eyes are wide with surprise, but there's a small smile on her face.

I laugh, although I'm not opposed. God knows I'm envious of Toby and his son every time I see them. "Not yet. I mean, I figure you should go back to teaching if that's what you want. Planning vacations together, hosting friends at our place, just the everyday things couples do."

She thinks it over, and I steel myself in case she says she's not ready for that step.

"I am getting bored at home. The more I try to remember, the more frustrated I'm becoming. Dr. Lipstein said something about that last week. I mean, he's told me that I may never remember, but last week he said I'll eventually need to put it aside and move forward with my life. If it happens, it happens."

"So?"

She twirls the glass between her fingers and watches the fluid swoosh around.

"What are you holding back?" I ask.

Her teeth nibble on her bottom lip and she looks at me. "Does this entail you moving into the master bedroom again?"

I blow out a breath and run my hand through my hair. If I'm going to ask her to move forward, then I need to take a step forward as well, no matter how painful that room is to me. "Yeah."

"Not just to sleep. Clothes in the closet, toiletries in the bathroom."

I nod. "Yes. I'm in."

She smiles. "Okay. So we're just going to put my memory issues aside and really start new?"

I put my hand on the nape of her neck, massaging the back of her scalp. "Yeah, we are."

I pull her toward me and kiss the holy hell out of her for the entire restaurant to witness. I'm finally back where I belong.

THAT NIGHT, Lucy's busy preparing dinner when I grab my clothes and hangers and head down the stairs to the master bedroom and hang them in the closet. Lucy's taken all the boxes and put them back in the hallway closet. I told her she can put them in an upstairs bedroom, but she said if we're starting new, then those need to be put away anyway.

Turning away from the closet I just put my clothes in, I stare at the bed then close my eyes, the memory of her leaving me forefront in my mind.

The night before, we'd been at one of the drawing nights at Northern Lights. We'd fought because I didn't want to go, but she was adamant we'd promised, so I went as always. I felt something was off with her but chalked it up to the fact that maybe her period was coming, or something was bothering her from work because she was still holding my hand, kissing my cheek. Hell, we'd actually had sex that night, even if she'd seemed overly emotional during it.

I woke up to her fully dressed, a suitcase at her side and tears streaming down her face.

"What's going on?" I asked. All I could think was that something had happened with her parents or her brother and they'd gotten back in touch with her.

"Adam, I'm not sure how to say this." She moved to the bedroom doorway and put her hand on the suitcase. My heart cracked—nothing good ever came from the start of a conversation like that. "I'm just not happy anymore."

"What?" I couldn't make sense of what she was saying.

She blinked and composed herself as if it took all her strength to say her next words to me. "I'm not happy anymore, and I'm... leaving you."

"You're leaving me?" I pulled the covers off me.

She put up her hand. "My decision is made. This is hard for me too, but we were young when we got married and I don't want this life anymore."

A hammer smashed my heart and I felt numb all over. "This life?"

"You and me. Sunrise Bay. I need to experience life more, and I can't do that here. I'm leaving."

I shook my head. "What the fuck are you talking about, Luce?"

Another tear slipped from her eye, and I rose from the bed, not understanding where any of it was coming from.

"Please don't." She stepped back. "I can't do this anymore, Adam. I'm so sorry. It's for the best."

Then she wheeled her suitcase out of the house. I rushed out of bed and realized I was naked, so I opened a drawer and put on shorts. I ran out of the room to go after her, but she must've had it all planned out because the front door was locked when I got there. By the time I got it open, she was in her SUV, the tires squealing as she drove away.

My ass fell to the stairs and I sat there for an hour, expecting her to come back, replaying what the hell had happened. And when I called a thousand times or more, she never answered. Every text I sent went unread. Eventually, I realized she'd meant what she said and wasn't coming back.

"Hey, you," Lucy says, coming into the room and wrapping her arms around my waist. "All moved in?"

She lays her cheek on my chest and I wrap my arms around her body, squeezing her to my side. Fuck, I wish I had the luxury of forgetting that moment like she did. It would make this a helluva lot easier.

"Dinner's ready." She looks up at me, her forehead creased with worry. "You okay?"

We agreed we'd be honest about everything, I remind myself. "There's a reason I didn't want to come in here."

"Why?"

"This is where it happened. This is where you told me you were leaving me."

Her jaw drops. "Oh. Adam, if you—"

I stop her with a kiss. "No. It's time to make new memories in here. I'll be better when I wake up tomorrow, I know it."

"Are you sure?"

She's still worried, I can tell. I nod. "Yeah."

She dislodges herself from me and sits on the edge of the bed. "I have something to tell you."

Panic flares inside and every nerve fires up a fight-or-flight response. I don't go to sit with her. I stand where I am and cross my arms. "What?"

"You know those nights at Northern Lights?" She bites her lip. Never a good sign.

"Yeah."

"Well, I guess Mrs. Pierce was a confidante for me. She told me I used to plan those nights so that you'd draw."

I release my arms and stare at her, not fully understanding.

"She told me that when she asked me to walk her to her room that night. I've been trying to figure out if that's why I left. She mentioned that some important person from the art world was going to call you, but you never responded. Could that have been the reason?"

I vaguely remember someone calling, but I was so deep in my anger phase, I told them off and hung up. "Really?"

She nods. "I'm sorry. I should've said something earlier. I just wanted to figure it out before I did. I found it in my journals. I guess you'd stopped drawing a year or so after we were married and I felt like you shouldn't let that part of you die, so I set up those nights at the retirement home. Are you mad?"

I blow out a breath and shake my head. "No. I'm not mad." I sit next to her on the bed and grab her hand. "But I told you, drawing isn't some big dream of mine I never fulfilled. I'm happy, Luce, I promise you."

Her eyes widen. "What?"

"You called me Luce."

I smile, since I didn't make a conscious decision to not include the "y". Nothing came to my mind to say she's not mine. "Don't feel guilty about me deciding to stay here. I'm where I want to be." I cradle her cheek.

"I really hope it's not why I left you. I mean, why would I do that?"

"Let's talk about that later," I say, nudging her to lie down. She crawls up the bed and my body looms over her, my lips finding hers. "Time to break this bed in again."

Her hands land on my cheeks, keeping my eyes on her. "What did I do so good in my life to win you twice?"

"I guess we're both just lucky."

She brings my face down to hers and we do a pretty damn good job of picking up where we left off. Unfortunately, dinner was ruined, but I was only hungry for Lucy anyway.

Chapter Twenty-eight

Lucy

"Crap," I say in the bathroom the next morning, spotting blood on my underwear. I should've known when that old familiar feeling of cramps woke me in the middle of the night that something was going on.

"What?" Adam's shadow is outside the door. "Are you okay?"

"Yeah, I just have some bleeding and I had some cramping last night."

"Is this your way of telling me you need me to go to the store and buy tampons? Because you just ruined my day."

I chuckle because I know he's joking. "I shouldn't get my period. Since I got the IUD, I haven't had one, other than a little spotting in the beginning."

He tries the doorknob, but I locked it. "Is this more serious? I'll call in to work."

I finish up in the bathroom, shoving toilet paper into my underwear since I have absolutely nothing here. I doubt Adam keeps sanitary items for his renters. When I open the door, Adam's sitting on the edge of the bed, his face pale white.

"What's wrong?" I ask.

"I don't like this. It sounds like you should go to the doctor and I should call in."

"I'm fine. I'll call my old doctor, and in the meantime, it's just a period. Who knows? It's not like I have blood gushing down my legs."

He cringes. "You sure?"

"I'm positive."

"I wasn't too rough last night?" He rises from the bed and places his hands on my hips, hovering over me.

I roll my eyes. "Relax. You know I enjoyed every minute of it." I give him a saucy smile.

He kisses me way more briefly than I want. "Okay. Call me though. Let me know what's happening. I'm training a new guy, so we'll be in the truck most of the day while I show him the trails and stuff."

I inch up on my toes and wrap my arms around his neck. "I'll keep you in the know."

"Good. There's a plate of eggs in the microwave for you."

"You're too good to me." I kiss him again, hating when we part.

"I know." He winks.

I playfully swat at him and fall back to my heels.

"Want me to grab you stuff before I go?"

I eye the clock. "No, you'll be late if you do. I might call Cora or one of the girls to take me into town. Maybe Cora can take me to the doctor."

"This weekend, we're getting you a car, okay?"

I nod because it's inevitable. Part of moving forward is getting me a car and continuing on with my life. "Sounds good. I'm going to call Principal Richards about maybe subbing and see if there are any openings for next year."

"That's great, but don't worry about anything financially. I've got us more than covered, okay? All the rent this place brought in, I put it in an account because it didn't feel right to spend it myself when this place was ours." He eyes me as though he's worried about my reaction.

I'm fine to talk about the past. I just wish I knew why I left him. Not because I doubt where we are, but I want to close that book and know whatever it was isn't hidden and waiting to come out and jeopardize our new beginning.

"I don't want you to pay for everything though. I want us to be a partnership."

He presses a soft kiss to my forehead. "We are. This is just my turn to hold the backpack, okay?" His thumb and forefinger linger on my chin, keeping my gaze glued to his. There's worry and trepidation in those hazel eyes.

"Okay," I say, but in order for me not to feel like a freeloader, I need to start getting my life on track.

He places a gentle kiss on my lips and walks toward the door.

"Adam?"

"Yeah?" He turns right before leaving the room. He's sexy as hell in his ranger uniform.

"Did I leave you my ring?" I slide my fingers over my bare left ring finger.

He opens his mouth but closes it. For a moment, I don't think he's going to answer. "You did. It's at my old house."

"Oh," I say, unsure if maybe he doesn't want to give it to me.

"We can pick it up tonight, but..."

"But?"

"Nothing." He smiles. "When I get home, we'll drive over there and get it."

"Great. I didn't want to ask in case you didn't want to give it to me."

He eats up the distance between us with a few long strides and his thumb and forefinger touch my chin again. "I want you to stay my wife, and you should have a ring on your finger that symbolizes that. I gotta go. Let me know about the doctor."

He kisses me again, his tongue sliding in my mouth this time. As always, it stirs a buzzing through my body that zeros in between my legs.

"Have a great day, dear," I say to his retreating back.

"Thanks, wife."

I wait for the door to shut before I grab my phone and call Cora to see if she can grab me before I call the doctor.

"Sorry, Luce, I'm taking Toby's mom into Anchorage," Cora says.

"I wish, but the inn is crazy right now," Mandi says when I call her.

I call every sister, and even Marla has some luncheon thing.

My phone rings before I can decide whether I should try someone else or just call an Uber.

"Hello?" I ask.

"I heard you're looking for a ride?" Ethel asks. I didn't have her number programmed in because I didn't know if she had a phone.

"Oh, yeah, I don't have an appointment at the doctor's yet, but I can just call an Uber."

"Nonsense, we're about to leave. We'll get some supplies, and I've already got you scheduled with Dori's granddaughter-in-law."

"I'm sorry?"

"Stella. She's squeezing you in as a favor to us. Be there in twenty." She hangs up.

I remember Dori mentioning that her granddaughter-in-law is a family doctor, so I search up my old gynecologist and call the office to get an appointment. The receptionist answers on the first ring and I explain my situation, hoping I can secure an appointment before Ethel and Dori get here.

"I'm sorry, Dr. Ramirez no longer has a practice here and we haven't found a replacement yet," she says. "Most of our patients are going to a new clinic in Lake Starlight that handles OB-GYN issues."

"You don't have any doctors there?"

"No one who specializes in that. I promise you'll love the clinic. People rave about it. I wish it had been around when I was having babies and raising them. Sadly, those years are gone now."

"Okay, well, I think someone I know got me an appointment with one of the physicians there, but I wanted to see Dr. Ramirez since she's familiar with me." Of course that was the old Lucy, not the new one.

"Go, sweetie. Promise you'll love it. I heard there's a waterfall in the waiting room," she whispers as though it's a secret.

"I don't have much of a choice, so I'll go. Thank you so much."

I hang up and go back to the bathroom to make sure I haven't leaked through the toilet paper. There isn't a ton of blood, so I get rid of it and put more in, hoping Ethel and Dori can take me to buy some pads.

As though they heard me, after I wash my hands and walk out of the bathroom, the doorbell rings. The sound of two arguing old ladies comes through the door.

I barely open the door before they shove in, Dori pushing a box in my stomach. "Here you go… oh, you were right, Ethel, this place is beautiful."

"They did so much work. It was horrible when they first moved in. I tried to give Adam a loan, but he wouldn't hear of it."

I listen, hoping a memory triggers, but when it doesn't, I look at the box they thrust at me. Super Plus Night Absorbency. Are these… bladder control pads?

I sigh, but I can't very well complain.

"I told her you weren't menopausal," Dori says.

"What? Are they too big?" Ethel asks, clutching her purse. "You should've seen the look the guy gave us, so we felt we had to explain."

"You told the guy at the drugstore that I needed pads and you selected these?" I hold them up, really hoping that when Nikki gets this news, she doesn't share. The last thing I need is for all of Sunrise Bay to think I don't have my memories or control of my bladder.

"We didn't say names." Ethel smiles.

I nod. "I'll be right back," I say through clenched teeth.

By the time I get the pad on, I understand what poor babies feel like. But it's better than toilet paper.

I come out and they're standing by the door with their hands in front of them like kids who were up to no good. I eye them suspiciously, but what could they have really done?

"Thank you for taking me."

"No problem. My Stella is the best." Dori walks out first.

I lock up and release a breath seeing the Cadillac in the driveway. "Do you want me to drive?"

Please say yes. Please say yes.

"Do you remember how to drive?" Dori asks.

"I do. Adam took me out already."

Dori throws her hand in the air. "She remembers how to drive but not me. I don't get it."

"I'm sorry," I say out of habit.

"Don't be sorry." Ethel rolls her eyes and pulls out the keys. "And I can drive. You relax in the back."

I smile and feel as if I should send Adam an "I love you" text as I slide in just in case I never return from this adventure.

Having no other choice, I buckle my seat belt and keep my eyes closed for the majority of the ride to Lake Starlight.

Chapter Twenty-nine

Lucy

The receptionist at Dr. Ramirez's old office was right. There is a waterfall in the middle of the reception area. There's also an entire area for kids to play, and the walls are painted to depict Dr. Seuss stories. Dori tries to go in the back, but the receptionist stops her. I politely give my name, and the receptionist smiles while telling me it'll be a moment.

"This is impressive," Ethel says, glancing around. "Stella and her partners did a great job."

Dori smiles proudly. "I know. You see those paintings in the children's area? My Liam did those."

"He's so talented."

"So who is Stella married to?" I lean forward to look at Dori. Although I've heard of the Baileys, I don't know them personally. Although after reading Buzz Wheel, the online gossip blog in Lake Starlight, sometimes I feel like I do.

"Oh, she's not married just yet. They'll be married next year. Kingston, my youngest grandson."

"The firefighter?" I ask.

She nods again, a proud smile overtaking her entire face. "They have the sweetest love story." She elbows Ethel and winks. "Another second chance young love story."

I'm sure these two feel as though they pushed Adam and me together, but I think we're just fated to be with one another.

A woman comes out of the back and says, "Lucy Greene?"

"I'll be back," I say, standing.

"Oh, we'll just go say a quick hello." Dori stands.

"I can do this myself. I'll tell Stella to come out." They walk over to the woman and give them my name.

I raise my hand behind them and the nurse smiles at me.

"Hey, Sarah." Dori walks through the door to the back without the nurse inviting her.

Obviously this isn't the first time Dori's barged in.

"Hi, Dori," Sarah says. "Why don't you two sit right out here and I'll check Lucy in? After Stella sees her, you two can come in and say hello." The nurse points at a seat for two near the nurses' station.

"I guess so."

Ethel and Dori sit down where they're told, already chatting with the other nurses about someplace called Sweet Infusion and their donuts.

"Thank you," I mouth to Sarah, then she leads me farther down the hallway.

"Step on the scale for me." She motions to a scale and I do as she asks. "We're used to Dori. We actually refer to that chair as her and Ethel's."

"Like a time-out chair?"

She laughs, jotting down my weight. "Pretty much. They don't much care for HIPPA guidelines. You should see when the Bailey kids come in. She's pushier than Ethel."

"Oh, just wait. Ethel will surprise you."

Sarah laughs and I follow her down the hallway to a room way too close to the Dori-and-Ethel chair. Ethel waves at me and I smile back. They'll probably have a glass to the door within minutes.

Once we're in the room, I go over my symptoms with Sarah and she gives me a gown to put on, leaving the room for me to disrobe.

I take off my clothes at warp speed and put on the gown, then sit on the bed with the paper blanket over my legs. I have no doubt Ethel and Dori won't sit there like altar boys and the last thing I want is to flash the entire office.

A soft knock on the door sounds a couple minutes later. I'm pleasantly surprised that I didn't have to wait long, but then Ethel's face pops through the opening. "We worried we missed her."

"Nope." I shake my head. "I'm pretty sure you'd see her before I would."

She's about to shut the door when a woman comes up behind her. "Ethel?"

"Stella!" Ethel opens the door wider and steps into the room, using the excuse that she had to let Stella in.

Stella is stunning. Her cheekbones are high and her dark umber skin glows. And of course when she smiles, the entire room lights up. No wonder she won over a Bailey. She's beautiful.

"I take it this is your granddaughter?"

"In-law," I correct.

"Oh, I think it's safe to say the in-law gets dropped in their minds." Stella hugs Ethel and leads her out of the room with a gentle hand on her back. "I'm just going to talk to Lucy for a minute. Why don't you join Dori on the chair?" She shuts the door behind Ethel.

"You're a master at that," I say.

She laughs, sanitizes her hands, and shakes mine. "I've had my fair share of practice, believe me. I'm Stella."

"Hi. Lucy." I smile.

"Nice to meet you. So tell me what's going on. I'm almost positive the call I received this morning isn't accurate." She sits at the computer and presumably pulls up my new patient file.

"I don't even want to ask what you heard."

She chuckles. "That you're bleeding, and you just recently got back together with one of Ethel's grandsons and she's worried he may have hurt you while you were having sex."

"Seriously?" My mouth drops open.

"The game of telephone with Dori and Ethel is a dangerous one, I assure you."

I shake my head.

"Why don't you tell me your version of what's going on?" Her soft smile sets me at ease.

"Okay, well, I have an IUD because I have bad periods and I haven't bled at all since the first month, but I had some bad cramping last night. And disclaimer, I did have sex with my husband, but I've been having sex with him for a while now, so I don't think that's it. And then I was bleeding this morning. I guess it kind of scared me."

She types away on the computer. "Who put your IUD in?"

"I was in Idaho."

She nods and types, then swivels her chair my way. "Why in Idaho? Did something happen or did you two recently move up to Alaska?"

My shoulders sag. "Well..."

I tell her my entire sordid story about leaving Adam and my memory loss and why they put the IUD in when I had always been on the pill previous to that. Eventually the conversation returns to Dr. Ramirez. Stella nods a lot and smiles when a nervous laugh escapes me. The story sounds made up, as though I'm talking about a book or some soap opera.

She stands afterward and pulls out the dreaded stirrups. "Okay, I'm going to do an exam on you. I've already asked Sarah to call over to Dr. Ramirez's office for your file. We've had a lot of patients come over from there, so we should be able to get it right away. This way we can see where things were a year ago."

"I can get my records from Idaho too if you need them. I'd just have to call my mom." Which I don't want to do, but I will.

"We might need them, but let's start here first. Since you can't remember your medical history, I want to make sure all is well today, and I can get Dr. Ramirez's files pretty quickly. If I don't find your IUD I'm going to send you down for a pregnancy test since there would be no way of knowing how long it's been out and you've been sexually active." She pops her head out of the room. "I'm just examining her now, ladies, so hold up a few minutes, okay?" She closes the door and turns to me again.

"Do you have a lock on that door?" I joke although I'm happy the table doesn't face the door at least.

"I'd need a dead bolt and an alarm to stop those two. I swear they're like elderly MacGyvers who can pick locks." She assists me with putting my legs up in the stirrups and asks me to slide down the table so far I fear I'm about to fall off. "Dori has some magic way of getting into one of my fiancé's sister's houses. It's a running joke in the family. She's caught them one too many times in the kitchen."

Listening to her talk relaxes me. After she finishes the exam, she slides back and takes off her gloves before helping me up.

"I don't see your IUD, which means it probably fell out."

"From having sex?"

She laughs. "More than likely not. It was probably already becoming dislodged and maybe that was the final thing to do it, but most times, there's not a reason. I want to make sure it's not in your uterus though, so I'm going to have you go to the ultrasound room. By the time you're done, I should have your records and we'll see where you want to go from here." She leans on the desk for a moment. "We could put in another IUD if you'd like, if everything's okay, or if you feel as though you'll remember the pill, we could choose that again. But just sit tight for a second while I arrange the ultrasound. We'll get this all sorted." She heads for the door but turns around. "And I'm not telling Ethel anything, so it's up to you if you want her to know." She winks like she understands what I'm going through.

Once she's gone, I hop down and grab my phone, messaging Adam that the IUD is missing and they're doing an ultrasound. He tells me to keep him informed and apologizes for Ethel and Dori, as always.

Sarah comes back in five minutes later and walks me to the ultrasound room. I'm still wearing the gown, and Ethel and Dori watch me pass.

"She has a nice figure," Dori says to Ethel.

"No wonder Adam can't keep his hands off her and they're in this predicament."

My face heats, but Sarah is nice enough to pretend she didn't hear them.

An ultrasound tech welcomes me into the darkened room and Sarah shuts the door when she leaves. Man, my vagina is getting the whole workup today. Last night it got plenty of attention from Adam, and now Stella's said hello. Soon the ultrasound tech, Kit, will pay her a visit. The joys of being a woman. Modesty has no place here.

Twenty minutes later, I'm back in the exam room, waiting for Stella and trying to decide if I should get another IUD or go back to the pill. The IUD was much easier than the pill, but if Adam and I want to start a family, then I don't need something semipermanent inside me. Though I'm probably rushing things thinking about kids. Hello, he was going to divorce me only seven weeks ago. But Adam's always wanted a family of his own. I could get the IUD out in a year. I shake my head, trying to clear my racing thoughts. I'll just ask Stella for guidance when she comes back.

Someone knocks on the door and Stella comes in, shutting the door behind her. She sits on her chair and I detect something different in her demeanor this time. She's not as smiley as she was the first time we met.

"So good news, we didn't see the IUD on the ultrasound. You more than likely dislodged it and maybe never saw it in the toilet."

"Last night?"

"My best guess is that it was at least a week or more ago, which is why you're spotting. Can I ask you a question, Lucy?"

I don't like how she asks that. I nod.

"Were you only on the IUD for period issues or was it for birth control?"

"Just to manage my period. I wasn't sexually active when I got it since I didn't even remember my husband at the time, but I am now. Oh god." My eyes flare and I clasp my hand over my stomach. "Am I pregnant? Did I miscarry? Is that what the cramps were?"

I stare at my stomach as though I should've known I had a baby in there. How do I tell this to Adam? He'll be devastated. I'm devastated.

"No. You're just having your period."

I blow out a relieved breath. "Oh, good. I mean, if I was pregnant, that'd be great too. I mean, Adam wants kids. I want kids. We both want kids." I force myself to stop rambling to allow her to talk.

Her smile softens and she walks over to me, reaching for my hand. "I received your medical history from Dr. Ramirez's office. Lucy, has anyone ever told you that you have endometriosis?"

"What?" I frown.

"It's a condition where tissue grows outside your uterus, and sometimes it can block your fallopian tubes. I know you had the accident and you don't recall this, but Dr. Ramirez met with you and sent you for a hysterosalpingogram test where dye is inserted into your vagina by a catheter. Then X-rays are taken to see where the dye goes. Lucy, your dye didn't freely go into the abdomen, which means you have blockages in both your tubes."

My stomach turns over. "Meaning?"

"Meaning that in order to conceive, you'd most likely be looking at fertility treatments and probably have to go straight to IVF. The problem with endometriosis is that we can go in and remove it, but it can come back. It leaves you at a high risk for an ectopic pregnancy, which is automatically not a viable pregnancy, plus it's a potentially life-threatening situation for the mother. Not to mention that if we didn't catch an ectopic pregnancy in time, you could lose an ovary and a fallopian tube." She pats my leg. "This is a lot of information for you to get all at once. Do you want me to have Adam come down or call Ethel in?"

I shake my head, coming out of a fog. "You said Dr. Ramirez told me this?"

"Yes, but obviously because of your accident, you don't remember. Now, I suggest just restarting the pill at this point. Let's have you go home, talk to Adam, then we'll get back together. There are some great surgeons and fertility treatments available."

"What are the chances of them being successful?"

She sighs. "You need to go through more tests, Lucy. More recent ones. Dr. Ramirez put your endometriosis at stage four. We need to see if surgery is even an option."

"How could I have not known this?"

"Well, you've had painful periods and the pills, and the IUD probably helped you with the pain. But sometimes women just don't feel it. The symptoms come and go, and most chalk it up to a stomach issue rather than a reproductive issue. But we'll figure this out."

"Can I see the notes from Dr. Ramirez?"

She hems for a moment. "Sure. They haven't been scanned in yet, so give me a second."

She leaves, and thank God Ethel doesn't try to come in. My phone pings in my purse, but I ignore it, hopping down to get dressed while I wait.

Stella returns right after I get my second shoe on. I stare at the date on my last visit with Dr. Ramirez and bile rushes up my throat. Last March.

"Thank you," I say.

I walk out of the room, past Ethel and Dori, past the

damn waterfall, and once I'm outside, I bend over and throw up in the trash can. I finally have the answer, but it's far from the one I wanted.

Lucy

I tell Ethel and Dori that I'm fine, I just have an upset stomach. On the way home, I hear the agitation in my voice when I have to explain what an IUD is.

All Ethel says is, "It stays there?"

They drop me home and I send Adam a message that we'll talk when he gets home, but that I'm fine.

Fine should be my new slogan. Just a T-shirt that says "I'm fine" so I can point at it when people ask.

I go out to the deck and call my mom. She answers on the fifth ring, which means she probably wasn't going to answer at all but couldn't help herself.

"Lucy," she says as if I'm a telemarketer.

"Did you know why I left Adam? You did, didn't you? You purposely kept this from me?"

"Luce," she says in the same way she has every time she's hidden something from me.

"Tell me!" I scream. "I have a right to know. Did you know that's why I left him?"

She's silent.

"There's my answer. How could you ever call yourself a mother? How could you let me come back here and rekindle things with him, knowing I can't give him the one thing he wants? Was it just to hurt him? Hurt the Greenes? Hurt me as punishment for staying?" I can't stop yelling as tears stream down my face.

All I can envision is despair and disappointment in the hazel eyes I love so much.

"I told you to come home. I didn't want you up there, but you were defiant like always. What was I to do?"

"Tell me! Tell me you knew why I left, so at the very least I could've told him before we fell back in love." I hate saying we fell back in love, because in my mind, I've always loved him.

"If he really loves you, Lucy, he'll understand this is out of your control."

"Mom!" I shake my head, unable to talk to her with the rage simmering through my veins. "I never want to talk to you again." I click end call.

Sitting on the patio chair, I bury my head in my hands. How on earth do I tell this to Adam? Explain why I left? Explain that there's a good chance he'll never get the large family he always wanted?

The years of my parents' own fertility problems come to mind. My mom's roller coaster of emotions every time she went to the doctor. The false hope that this time might be it. The cost of treatments that put them in debt. My dad never being home because he was working three jobs to try to pay for the treatments. The vision of my mom's back bruised on both sides as my dad tried to find a spot to poke her again. I close my eyes, understanding why the old Lucy ran. But I'm not sure why she didn't talk to Adam about it.

I need my fucking journal.

I go into the closet and thumb through my journals. But I've read everything and there wasn't anything about us trying to have a baby. Why would Dr. Ramirez even test me for it? After an hour, I come up empty once again. I wish I knew what I had been thinking that day. Why I would leave the only man who could get me through the devastating news?

For the first time in a long time, all I want to do is bury myself in the bed and wish this was just a nightmare.

I message Adam that I won't be fixing dinner and he makes a joke about it being my time of the month. I strip down and put on my pajamas before sliding into bed.

"Luce," Adam says, the weight of his body dipping the mattress. "You feeling okay?" He places the back of his hand on my forehead.

I turn toward him. He's got his work shirt off, leaving him in his gray undershirt. I stare at him, reaching for him.

"What is it? You need some pain meds? I stopped at the store. Got you what you used to use and a new heating pad since I may have thrown away your old one." He winces.

"Thanks."

Then he opens his arms for me to crawl into and holds my head to his chest, my legs sliding between his.

"How was work?" I ask.

"Ah, the guy I'm training needs some common sense training, but uneventful."

I sigh and tighten my arms around him, tears coming fast and hard. I'm unable to control them. How did the old me ever pretend everything was okay?

"Whoa." He dips his head back, but I nuzzle my head harder into his chest and he holds me tighter. "It's okay. What's wrong? Was there a near-miss with Grandma Ethel and Dori? I knew I should've called in."

I shake my head and pull back, rising up on my knees.

He lies on the bed, one hand grasping mine as though he's afraid I'm going to run away. Which, oddly enough, never even came to mind this time around.

"You're scaring me," he says, his voice rough.

"Adam, did we ever discuss having kids?"

He maneuvers our hands so that he's winding his fingers with mine. I already know the answer before he says, "Sure. We were married."

"No, I mean closer to the time I left. Were we trying?"

He sits up quickly. "Did you remember something?" The excitement on his face makes me feel terrible.

I shake my head. "No."

He looks away for a moment. "Well, we wanted them. Especially after Cora got pregnant with Brody. You know how it is, the teenage fantasy of having your kids grow up with our best friends' kids. You went off the pill a few months before you left, but I mean, we weren't disappointed when you'd get your period or anything. We weren't taking temperatures and you weren't putting your legs over your head like you see in movies."

"Yeah, that makes sense."

He sits with his back to the headboard and grabs my hands. "You have something to tell me. I can tell."

I nod and tears break free once more.

"Oh, Luce, you know I'm here for you."

I wait until my breathing evens out and figure I just need to get it all out in the open. What happens, happens. "I found out why I walked out on you today."

His eyes widen. "So you did remember?"

I shake my head and he tilts his, understandably confused.

"Turns out that around the time I left, I was seeing Dr. Ramirez and I had some tests done which I'm assuming was behind your back." I swipe my tears away with the back of my hand. "I found out today that I can't have kids. Well, I might be able to, but not without fertility treatments. I also found out right before I left you, I just didn't remember."

"What? Are you sure?" He searches my face, and I see the pain I expected in his hazel eyes.

I nod. "I'm sure."

"We should go for a second opinion."

I look him straight in the eye. "The doctor today was my second opinion. She looked at the same results Dr. Ramirez did. That's why I left you, Adam. Because I couldn't bear your children. I understand if you want to leave me now. I can't give you what you want."

He's silent, brooding, as his gaze digs into mine. "Do you want to leave me?"

"I want you to have the life you've always wanted. The one you deserve."

"You're what I want, Luce. You. That's all."

I sigh and bury my head in a pillow. I really want to scream in it, but I hold back. "I know you want a big family. You've always made that known."

"You said fertility treatments are an option. There might be a chance."

"Do you know how much it costs? And the chances are so slim. It tears happy couples apart. I saw it with my parents. Even after they had Zane, they never got back to who they were as a couple, the love they had for one another. I could never go through that with you."

He slides out of the bed. "What are you saying?" The edge in his voice scares me.

"I don't want to do fertility treatments, but I also don't want you to wake up one day and resent me. First I took away your opportunity to play football, then your drawing—"

"Jesus, we're back to that!" he yells. "I told you I'm happy where I am."

I roll over on the other side of the bed, standing. "I still took it away from you."

He clenches his jaw and looks away. "When are you ever going to understand? I only want you." His shoulders fall and he shakes his head. "I only want you."

"You say that now, but you'll feel differently watching Brody and all your nieces and nephews grow up." All of a sudden, all those emotions I must've felt last year rush up inside me. I understand her, the old Lucy. I understand how she could've left him. "It's better to have you hate me now than to resent me in ten years." God, those words sound so familiar.

"What? You said we'd fight this time. You said you were in this. But only until it got tough, huh?" His face grows red.

"I've seen it, Adam. It's not pretty, okay? Couples going through infertility with such a low chance of success. You think the odds are great until they're stacked against you. How many years would we do it, put in money we can't afford, to try, and then say we're done, never having gotten what we wanted out of it. I guarantee by that time, our relationship will be damaged beyond repair. And adoption? Another long, hard road."

"Then we fight. We fight to keep us alive." His screams echo off the walls.

Tears burst out of me. "How do you know our love is strong enough to endure all this?"

"Because it is." His voice lowers and he rounds the bed. "Because my life without you wasn't a life. And now that I have you back, I'm not going to lose you."

"No, you're going to lose the life you dreamed of," I say.

"I have you. And if we really want kids, we'll figure out a way to make it happen. I have no doubt we'll get through this. Somehow. Someway. We might have a few scrapes and bruises, but you'll always have my arms to run to. You said this is a partnership, so I'll keep you up when you're down and vice versa, but running isn't an option."

"I'm not going to run. I told you, didn't I?"

He puts his arms around me. "You sounded like you were about to run."

"It's tempting. I feel like such a failure. I'm the one who ran out on you, the one who has amnesia, and now the one who can't give you a child." I cry into his chest, the despair making me exhausted. "I can't help but fear one day you'll think you'd have had an easier life with someone else."

He runs his hand down my hair and holds me. I sob, unable to stop all the emotions from everything over the last three months escaping.

"Time to lie down," he says gently and leads me to the bed. He shrugs off his pants before climbing in and holding me. "This is fresh news. We just need to worry about this one step at a time, but right now, let's relax."

He holds me, his hands running up and down my back and hip. Eventually my tears run dry and my eyes drift closed.

Chapter Thirty-one

Adam

I slide out from Lucy, leaving her in bed, and put on a pair of track pants before heading into the kitchen to grab a beer. It's late now, nearing midnight. The sun has just set, so I walk out onto the deck and head down to the firepit. After I get the fire started, I sit in a chair and drink my beer.

I've never felt more hopeless in my life. It makes me feel like when I watched my dad try to grab my mom up through the ice and the panicked look on his face when he came up with nothing.

Now, the woman I love is mourning her chance to bear a child—at least to bear one as easily as I think women imagine. I understand what she's talking about with the fertility treatments. I've heard the stories from my coworker, Nick. It was costly and time-consuming and an emotional roller coaster for him and his wife. But I have to believe we can get through this. Still, I have no magic wand to turn this around or make it easier for us. And I fear, as she does, that we have a long battle ahead of us.

But it's a relief to know the reason she left me. This I can deal with a lot easier than if she'd left me for another man.

I stare into the flames, wondering what our future will be like.

Lucy's not wrong—I want a big family. Ever since my mom died and we spent those first years without her, I knew that when I got older, I wanted it again. Not that we weren't still a family, but it was different. When Marla and my dad married, our lives morphed again. I love all my stepsiblings as much as I love my blood siblings, but I've always wanted that family like the one we had when my mom was alive.

Now I have to imagine my life with the possibility of not having kids. It's not a life I'd choose, but life without Lucy is far more horrid to think about. I already know how devastating that life is and I'm not willing to go back to it.

A creak on the stairs grabs my attention and I look to find Lucy coming down the steps, wearing my slides and my ranger coat. That is what family looks like. That image right there is what I want my future to be.

She walks over to me and crawls into my lap, placing her head on my shoulder. "I'm sorry."

I run my hand down her hair and kiss her forehead. "You have nothing to be sorry for."

"I shouldn't have tried to push you away." She sits up in my lap. "We agreed to do this together."

"Yeah, we did."

She lays her head back down on my shoulder and we both stare at the fire, mesmerized by the intensity of the flames.

"Do you feel at peace now?" she whispers over the crackle of the flames. "Now that we know why I left?"

"A small part of me does, but I'm more worried about you now." I kiss her forehead again, wishing I had some magic potion to make her feel better.

"What was your worst fear?"

"That you left me for someone else, he broke your heart, and you went to your parents knowing you couldn't come back here. You?"

"Similar. That you had another girl and I found out and left. But deep down, I think I knew that wasn't the case."

"Hey, Luce." I wait for her to turn her head and look at me. "We're going to get through this."

She nods. "I know. It's just a really hard thing to hear."

I'm not quite sure I believe that she thinks it will be okay, but for tonight, I won't pressure her.

THE NEXT MORNING, Lucy's face is red and slightly swollen from a night of crying, but she seems in slightly better spirits. At least she's not trying to run out on me.

"Hey, you going to be okay here on your own?" I ask, dressed for work. "I can call in."

"No." She tilts her head up from the side of the couch and I bend down to kiss her. "I'll be fine."

"And you'll be here when I get home?" It's taking a lot of trust for me to go to work today and set aside the fear that I'll return to an empty house.

"Promise." She smiles and it almost reaches her eyes. Good sign.

"Okay, I'll check in periodically."

"You don't have to, but I do enjoy hearing your voice." She laughs and the sound is nice to hear.

I leave the house and shed my jacket in the car, driving

over to my old childhood home. What Lucy doesn't know is that I'm going to propose to her again tonight with her ring. I have no grand plan, which sucks, but hopefully something will come to me. I don't want to involve my sisters, that's for sure. But I want Lucy to know that even with everything on the table, I still choose her and she chooses me.

"Why are so many of them home?" I mumble, seeing everyone's damn trucks in the driveway.

I climb out and I hear voices in the back yard, so I follow the noise to find Jed, Fisher, and Cameron out back, playing with a pen full of puppies.

"Are you guys going into the breeding business?" I ask.

Cameron turns to me. "Nope, Gunner's girl had her first set of puppies," he says like a proud father.

I forgot his yellow lab had gotten another dog pregnant. The family doesn't want anything to do with them and said that as soon as the puppies were old enough to leave their mother, they were going to him. Cameron happily agreed.

"What are you going to do with them?" I ask.

"I have no clue. Want one?"

"Hell no. I have no time for a dog."

I walk into the house through the back door and up the stairs to my old childhood bedroom, before we moved into the big house. I spent a year of my life here, missing her every day. Even after I thought I'd moved on, I hadn't.

I go into my drawer and reach in the back for her wedding ring. The one she left on the counter for me to find after she told me she was leaving. I wanted to throw it in the bay, but something in my gut told me to keep it, so I did. Thank goodness. Although I would buy her a new one. I thought maybe I should, since she's doing all the old Lucy, new Lucy stuff, but she's still *my* Lucy.

I put the ring in my pocket and head back downstairs

and out the back door. I have to get to Twisted Stem to get flowers and figure out a great proposal to show her how much I love her. Everything I think of doesn't seem to make a big enough statement that if we only have each other for the rest of our lives, I'll still be a happy man.

"Come on, I bet Lucy would love a dog," Cameron says when I come outside.

The group has gotten bigger, and I glance at the driveway to make sure I can get out. Presley's holding a dog to her chest and Cade's giving Cameron the death glare. Chevelle must've come with them because she's watching while Fisher's trying to get one to sit. The thing is, like, nine weeks old probably.

"Yeah, no," I say and begin to walk away, but then I get an idea.

"Only your dog would get someone's dog pregnant at the dog park. Why didn't you get him fixed?" Chevelle asks, sitting while one of the puppies follows her finger.

"Because I'm not cutting his balls off. As a man myself, I couldn't do it."

"Then don't take him to the dog park," Chevelle snips.

"Women love men with dogs."

She rolls her eyes at him. "One dog, Cam, not seven."

I head back over to the little playpen thing and pick up a yellow one with darker ears.

"I might be the stupidest man ever," I mumble to myself. "I'm taking one for you, Cam."

"That'll be two grand." He holds out his hand.

"Yeah, right," I say.

"Puppies are a hot commodity. But..." He waves me off. "You're like a brother, take him."

"You're not really going to sell them, are you? You know

you need breeder paperwork, and since the mother's family has abandoned them..." Chevelle keeps going.

Cameron raises his hand, opening and closing it because she won't stop lecturing him.

"Congrats to Lucy. At least *she's* getting a dog." Presley turns a cold look on Cade.

"We're busy. We both run businesses. We have no time for a puppy," Cade argues.

"Fine, I'll be in the truck waiting. Next time don't bring me." Presley huffs and stomps off toward the truck.

"Goddamn you, Cam." Cade runs a hand through his hair. "Give it back to me."

"Two grand please." Cam holds out his hand.

"Fuck off. I'll be sending you the bill when it eats my fucking couch." Cade grabs the dog Presley had and stomps over to his truck.

Presley's eyes are already widening in happiness.

"No refunds and no returns," Cam shouts.

I head away from the group with the puppy that'll probably work my patience until it's trained. As I drive to downtown, my entire plan comes to my mind.

Chapter Thirty-two

Lucy

I groan when there's a knock on the door. The last thing I want is to deal with anyone today . I love Ethel and Dori, but I really hope it's not them.

I mute the television and go to open the door. I'm shocked to find my mom, her arms crossed and a sour look on her face.

Great. This is exactly what I needed right now. Not.

"Can I come in?" she asks.

I hold out my arm and step out of her way. She did fly up here from Idaho after all. "Suit yourself."

I go back to the couch and sit, waiting for her to join me. She sits in the chair across from me and places a journal on the coffee table. I glance at her, and she nods to confirm it's what I think it is. The journal I've wanted since the beginning of my search.

"How could you—"

She puts up her hand. "I'm sorry, Lucy. I thought I was protecting you by keeping it. After your accident, I was in your room, grabbing clothes to wash and straighten up. I found it and I'm ashamed to say I read it."

"So you knew when we came here?" Anger boils inside me that she'd hide the journal. I'd explicitly asked about it multiple times, so she can't even pretend keeping it from me was a lie of omission.

"I did, and I don't expect you to forgive me, but just hear me out. Our relationship has been strained since you started hanging out with Adam when you were a child. I have feelings about that family that go way back. And when your dad and I told you our objections, they took you under their wing and you became closer than ever with them. I was jealous of Marla. I hated that woman for sitting in my role. My resentment grew and I don't know..." She throws up her hands in front of her. "I let too much time go by. I was too stubborn to admit that I saw what you and Adam shared. But when you came home and didn't want to talk about why you'd left, I figured I'd been right all along and all that time I'd mourned your absence was forgotten." She nods toward the journal. "When I read why you left Adam, I thought you made the right decision."

"But I didn't—"

"You didn't." She shakes her head. "I know that now. The way he's stuck by you with the amnesia and agreed to start a relationship with you without knowing why you left him says a lot about the love you share. Although I hate to admit it, I thought of course he'd push you aside to find someone who could give him children." She stares at her fingers. "I know the toll infertility can cause a couple. I wanted to spare you the pain."

"But it would've come up if and when I found someone else."

"True, but I felt if you left Adam because of that,

knowing how much you love him, it was because it was so important to him. Do you remember leaving now?"

I shake my head. "I found out from the doctor."

"Then hopefully when you read the journal entry, you'll understand a little bit of why I made the decision I did."

I pick up the journal, the weight of it heavy in my hands. I'm almost scared to read what I wrote.

"I thought about just mailing it, but I want you to know how sorry I am. I'm your mother, and I never should've let this get so out of hand. In some weird way, I convinced myself I was doing right by trying to protect you, but I was wrong." She stands. "I'll leave you to it. I'm at the inn if you want to talk. Otherwise, I'm flying back home tomorrow morning. I understand it might take you a while to forgive me, maybe you never will, but I hope you do." She gives me a sad smile, unshed tears in her eyes.

I go to stand, but she shoos me back down. "I'll see myself out." She walks toward the door but turns around before she leaves. "And Lucy, fertility treatments have improved since we were trying for Zane. I know after what you said in there what you're worried about, but you're strong enough. Look at you right now... you came here, faced your fears with Adam, and it all turned out okay. Who's to say the same won't happen again?"

She turns and I hear the door click shut a second later.

I hold the journal tightly and walk outside to the deck, sit at the patio table, and find my last entry.

I did it and I feel worse than I've ever felt in my life. I left Adam this morning with nothing more than a weak excuse about me not being happy. I'm such a chickenshit. But I know that my inability to give him a child would only tear us apart at some point. I saw what fertility treatments did to my parents' marriage and my heart would never be able to handle that happening to

Adam and me. I told myself when I drove away that I loved him enough to let him go. Even when I stopped at the base of the mountain and second-guessed myself. It took every ounce of willpower not to do a U-turn and run back into his arms. Adam's suffered enough loss in his life after his mom's death. And I've already taken a career involving his drawing and college football away from him. I couldn't take away his chance at having his own family too. His words the night we decided to try to conceive still ring in my ear. How excited he was to be a dad and have a family of his own. We argued about whether it'd be a boy or girl and if it was a boy, whether he'd have the Greene football genes. He joked that we'd be the favorites because we'd give Grandma Ethel her first great-grandbaby.

God, I miss him so much my heart aches. But it's better this way. I'd rather him hate me now than resent me in the years to come when all our spare rooms are empty. I know if I told him, he'd insist that we could be happy, but it would just be yet another thing I've taken from him. I'm tired of taking. I look at this as though I'm giving him a chance at the life he deserves and wants. Even if it's killing me to do it, I have to stay strong.

This is my last journal entry because there's nothing I want to write about anymore. I'm not going to depress myself more by staring at a blank page with a pen in my hand. So, wish me luck wherever life takes me.

I shut the book even though I want to read more. I roll over in my mind what I just read as I stare into the trees. I understand why I did it. The guilt that's consumed me since I found out yesterday is greater than anything I've ever had to bear. Even losing my memory. I'm disappointing the person I love the most. Isn't it normal to want to give my husband a child? To see him cry holding our baby for the first time? If I attack this journey of infertility, I have to prepare myself for disappointment because it just might not happen. But Adam is right—we need to fight for us, fight for our family. We've come way too far not to.

I'm so distracted with my thoughts that it takes me a few seconds to register the feeling of soft fur brushing along my ankles. I look down and find a puppy with a giant peony attached to its collar and a box that says, "Open me."

"Where did you come from?" I laugh and pick up the puppy and look over my shoulder, not finding anyone.

Opening the box, I find my wedding ring nestled inside. It's shiny and bright and looks brand new.

"Did I tell you about Cam's dog?" Adam comes out of the house and leans against the railing in front of me. He glances at the journal on the table but only gives it a fleeting look. "He got a dog at the dog park knocked up. Just chased her down and mounted before anyone could stop them."

"Really?" I pet the little puppy. It's so cute.

"We all know Cam can't raise a squad of puppies. They'd follow in their dad's footsteps and then there'd be puppies running all over Sunrise Bay. So this little guy needs a mommy and daddy and I figured we could use some practice. Plus, a little pet therapy while we set forth on our new journey."

I pick up the puppy and chuckle at what I find.

"But first..." He walks over and plucks the ring from my finger before falling down on bended knee. "We need to get remarried. I loved our first wedding, but I need to marry this Lucy. Not the old or new, just the Lucy who got me to fall in love with her twice in a lifetime." He winks.

"There's one problem here," I say.

He looks at me skeptically.

"Our little boy is actually a little girl."

He shakes his head with a smile. "All I care is that she's healthy."

"Good answer."

He holds the ring. "What do you say, Lucy Greene? Marry me again?"

"I'd marry you every day for the rest of my life." I try to blink away my building tears.

He slides the ring on my finger, stands, and bends over, kissing me until the puppy starts licking our chins. "Are you sure you want kids? Because if I'm gonna be cockblocked…"

I fist his shirt and tug him toward me, smashing his lips to mine.

Life doesn't get much better than this. I don't need all my memories to know that.

Adam

One Year Later

Lucy and I walk into Truth or Dare Brewery the night before tourist season begins in Sunrise Bay. It's packed as usual, but Lucy laughs from seeing a bunch of Lucy Takes Flight on the tables.

"What's up, Molly?" I ask while she pours Lucy's favorite, Melting Heart, and slides it her way. And then pours my favorite, No Stout for You.

"Nothing, just got back from Las Vegas on the red-eye this morning and I'm exhausted."

"Oh yeah, girls' trip. How fun," Lucy says.

I swing my arm around Lucy's shoulders and pull her closer. "Not more fun than hanging out with me and fruity umbrella drinks though, right?"

We flew back from the Caribbean yesterday, and let's just say we didn't see much of the beach. But it was our second honeymoon and well worth it. We opted to get remarried before tourist season—and looking at how full this room is, that was a smart choice. The regular tourists have clued into the fact that there's a party before their usual arrival and have started arriving earlier every year.

"Your tan looks great," Molly says. "I got stuck inside a casino the entire time."

I glance at Lucy and she hits me in the stomach. A little fact about their girls' trip came out just before we left the Caribbean. I have no idea how the news never reached up here, but it's taking everything in me not to tell someone. I mean, the queen of gossip in Sunrise Bay turning into the subject of gossip herself? It can't get any better than that, can it?

Molly goes down the bar to help someone else, and I slide a stool out for Lucy. We decided to not do anything baby related this past year and enjoy a year of being just the two of us without the pressure of starting a family. I think we needed it after our year apart. Plus, Lola, our little pup, had to learn not to use the house as her potty. She's still not perfect, but she's not getting knocked up at the dog park either.

"So what do you think? Ready for what's coming?" Lucy asks me.

We've already had a conversation about the upcoming fertility treatment process, and Stella gave us some great references in Anchorage.

"Yeah. I'm ready." I lean in and kiss her temple.

We needed this year to grieve the loss of how we thought becoming parents would go and to solidify us to face a new challenge. But regardless, we're starting the process next week.

"Hey, are you coming to talk to the class on Monday?"

Lucy's back at teaching. She loves her job and she's settled in well.

"Hey, you're back." Presley sits next to Lucy and they chat about our honeymoon.

Presley and Cade are due to get married next month. No one saw any issue with us pushing our wedding ahead of theirs since we were already married and kept it to immediate family only. Which, with my family, is a lot of people. Susan, Lloyd, and Zane came up from Idaho too. This time around, Lloyd gave Lucy away. Things aren't perfect between her family and me, but it's better than it was.

When I came home that day with Lola a year ago, I found Susan in our driveway, tears falling down her cheeks while she sat in her car.

After I proposed to Lucy, I told her to forgive her mom. To give her a chance. You only have one mom and I know what it's like to lose her. We went to the inn and had a tense and awkward dinner, but it was a step in the right direction.

"How's Bernie?" I ask Cade, trying to hold back my laugh.

He rolls his eyes. "I'm hiring another dog trainer. He's chewing the deck. What the hell?"

I laugh. Lola is so chill we haven't had a ton of issues with her, whereas Bernie should've been named Cujo.

"It's not fucking funny. Fucking Cam messaging Presley about those damn dogs." He shakes his head.

I clasp him on the shoulder. "Good luck, man, you've got years with that dog."

"I don't know. He might run away." He smiles, but Presley hears him and the girl's got a death stare that would scare Satan.

"So how was the girls' trip?" Presley asks Molly when she comes over and pours a few beers.

"You can't come behind here and pour your girl a beer?" she asks Cade.

"I'm paying you to do it," he says.

"What's up, guys?" Jed comes out from the back with a quesadilla in his hand. He slides it between Lucy and Presley. "For my favorite sisters-in-law."

"We're your only sisters-in-law and technically I'm not official yet," Presley says.

"We don't need a marriage license to make you family." Jed walks away into the crowd.

Mandi, Posey, Clara, and Xavier walk in, and we move to the table by the window so we have more room. It's only a matter of time before the rest of the Greenes join us.

"Where's Nikki?" Mandi asks. "I want details on the Vegas trip."

"You don't want details on our trip?" I ask.

"Why would we wanna hear how many orgasms you gave each other?" Posey says. "The rest of us aren't in serious relationships."

Lucy's hand finds mine under the table. I kind of wish we were at home alone.

The rest of our family arrives, Hank and Marla coming in last. Marla has a hairdo that suggests they were fooling around somewhere. They like to go to the football stadium and make out, which is embarrassing as fuck. I mean, they own a huge house, get your kinks there. Poor Rylan.

Marla goes right to Molly. "Where's Nikki? I need to talk to her."

I hit Lucy on the thigh under the table and she grabs my hand, squeezing it. She's adamant that this isn't our business to share, but Nikki's the one who had everyone in Sunrise Bay stopping Lucy to remind her about her past.

Sadly, Lucy hasn't had too many more memories resurface. Dr. Lipstein gave her hope that she might one day, not to count it out, but she's accepted it may never happen. I told her we'll make new, better memories anyway.

"Oh, what did you need?" Molly asks. I can tell she knows exactly why Marla wants to speak to Nikki.

How long did Nikki think she could keep something like this hidden?

Lucy pokes me in the stomach, and I look away from Marla and Molly. My wife glares at me. I relent and turn around to join the conversation with the rest of my siblings. We shoot the shit—Jed complains about the tuxedo he has to wear for Cade's wedding, Posey volunteers to do everyone's hair, and I order Lucy honey barbeque wings.

A half hour later, I spot Nikki walking through the square toward the brewery. When she comes inside, she heads straight to the bar and whispers something to Molly. Molly eyes Marla and they whisper again.

I slap Lucy's thigh to tell her it's coming. She rolls her eyes, giving me that damn look again. How can she not be as excited as I am? This is the kind of shit siblings live for. I wish I could've told Cade. He's gonna love this.

"Nikki." Marla stands, but a group of people get in her way.

Nikki has a panicked look on her face now and I'm about to burst out laughing until Lucy pinches me on the thigh.

"What the hell?" I ask.

"Can you two really not keep your hands off one another?" Chevelle says across the table.

"What do you care what they're doing?" Cam chimes in —because he does every time Chevelle speaks.

Jed hands Molly a stack of empty glasses then comes over. "Holy shit, you're never going to believe who just walked in."

"Oh God, do I even want to know?" Clara asks. "Someone from high school?"

"No." Jed glances back at the door.

I follow his vision to a big guy walking toward the bar.

"Nikki, we pay Molly to work. You realize that, right?" Cade says, not paying attention to Jed. He's gonna miss this moment.

"Nikki!" Marla waves. "We need to talk."

"Logan Stone," Jed says.

"Who's Logan Stone?" Posey asks.

"The MMA fighter?" Xavier says, glancing around now.

"No shit!" Cam turns to see him. "Why would he be in Sunrise Bay?"

Chevelle turns and finds Logan Stone in the crowd too. "Oh, he's a hottie."

That earns her a glare from Cam.

"You know what, Cade, just leave me be. She's still working, and I need her advice. That's what bartenders do, right?" Nikki snips at Cade.

"Hey, Nik," Molly says, her eyes growing wide when she sees Logan.

Nikki puts up her hand at her friend.

"You just had a girls' weekend. Why do you need to talk to her so bad?" Cade asks. "Not everything is urgent."

"Nik," Molly says again.

Logan Stone is right behind her now.

Jed can't lift his mouth off the floor and Xavier and Cam are ogling the man. I hit Lucy on the thigh again. She glances behind her, rolling her eyes at my excitement about what's about to go down.

"Nik," Molly says louder this time.

"What?" Nikki asks, and Molly points behind her.

Nikki slowly turns around and stares at the man behind her. I've never seen my sister look so panicked.

Jed finally lifts his jaw off the floor. "Hey, man, can I help you with something?"

Logan shakes his head, his eyes never leaving Nikki.

"Who is this guy?" Mandi asks Nikki.

"I'm her husband," Logan says and the entire restaurant quiets.

#karma

The End

ALSO BY PIPER RAYNE

The Baileys

Lessons from a One-Night Stand (FREE)

Advice from a Jilted Bride

Birth of a Baby Daddy

Operation Bailey Wedding (Novella)

Falling for My Brother's Best Friend

Demise of a Self-Centered Playboy

Confessions of a Naughty Nanny

Operation Bailey Babies (Novella)

Secrets of the World's Worst Matchmaker

Winning my Best Friend's Girl

Rules for Dating Your Ex

Operation Bailey Birthday (Novella)

The Greene Family

My Twist of Fortune (Free Prequel)

My Beautiful Neighbor (FREE)

My Almost Ex

My Vegas Groom

A Greene Family Summer Bash (Novella)

My Sister's Flirty Friend

My Unexpected Surprise

My Famous Frenemy

A Greene Family Vacation (Novella)

My Scorned Best Friend

My Fake Fiancé

My Brother's Forbidden Friend

A Greene Family Christmas (Novella)

Lake Starlight

The Problem with Second Chances

The Issue with Bad Boy Roommates

The Trouble with Runaway Brides

The Drawback of Single Dads

Plain Daisy Ranch

One Last Summer

The One I Left Behind

The One I Stood Beside

The One I Didn't See Coming

Modern Love

Charmed by the Bartender

Hooked by the Boxer

Mad about the Banker

Single Dads Club

Real Deal

Dirty Talker

Sexy Beast

Hollywood Hearts

Mister Mom

Animal Attraction

Domestic Bliss

Bedroom Games

Cold as Ice

On Thin Ice

Break the Ice

Chicago Law

Smitten with the Best Man

Tempted by my Ex-Husband

Seduced by my Ex's Divorce Attorney

Blue Collar Brothers

Flirting with Fire

Crushing on the Cop

Engaged to the EMT

White Collar Brothers

Sexy Filthy Boss

Dirty Flirty Enemy

Wild Steamy Hook-up

The Rooftop Crew

My Bestie's Ex

A Royal Mistake

The Rival Roomies

Our Star-Crossed Kiss

The Do-Over

A Co-Workers Crush

Hockey Hotties

Countdown to a Kiss (Free Prequel)

My Lucky #13 (FREE)

The Trouble with #9

Faking it with #41

Tropical Hat Trick (Novella)

Sneaking around with #34

Second Shot with #76

Offside with #55

Kingsmen Football Stars

False Start (Free Prequel)

You Had Your Chance, Lee Burrows

You Can't Kiss the Nanny, Brady Banks

Over My Brother's Dead Body, Chase Andrews

Chicago Grizzlies

On the Defense (Free Prequel)

Something like Hate

Something like Lust

Something like Love

The Nest

Mr. Heartbreaker

Mr. Broody

Mr. S (Title to be revealed)

Mr. C (Title to be revealed)

Holiday Romances

Single and Ready to Jingle

Claus and Effect

Merry Kissmas

Cockamamie Unicorn Ramblings

AMNESIA! That was our excitement level when we were plotting out The Greene Family Series and decided we were going to conquer a trope we've been dying to write. We're both lovers of the amnesia trope but haven't been able to find a book to make it work. Then came Adam and Lucy and voila, amnesia! To say we've been excited to write this for a while is an understatement.

So, what changed from the plotting to page? Well, not a whole lot. Surprise, right? For us too. We did take some fictional liberties when it came to Lucy's amnesia for romance reasons and we're okay with that. When we came up with the storyline that she couldn't have children being the reason she left, we had to do heavy research since it came as a surprise to her. Plus, we loved that we could bring in Stella from The Baileys series. LOL This time, our plotting worked out well but we're probably in a deficit if you added up all our books.

We hope you enjoyed Adam and Lucy's story. Infertility is a tough subject to handle in fiction. As some of you may know, Rayne went through it herself for years before she was blessed with twins. It's one of the darkest times of her life. The tests, the shots, the disappointment. Even when you finally hear the wonderful words, "you're pregnant", every milestone up to the delivery of a healthy baby or babies, you're waiting for that pin to drop, for something to go wrong. But on the flip side, the science of infertility treatments gives so many couples the opportunity to be parents, so there's the happiness too. Okay, enough on that subject, we write romcoms, right? LOL

We'd be nowhere without the great people below!

Danielle Sanchez and the entire Wildfire Marketing Solutions team.

Cassie from Joy Editing for line edits.

Ellie from My Brother's Editor for line edits.

Shawna from Behind the Writer for proofreading.

Hang Le for the cover and branding for the entire series.

Wander Aguiar for his awesome job of photographing our Adam and Lucy.

Bloggers who consistently carve out time to read, review and/or promote us.

Piper Rayne Unicorns who love our characters like we do!

Readers who took the time to read our story when there's so many choices out there. We are forever grateful! <3

As you read, Nikki's up next! Married to an MMA fighter? Yummy! The Sunrise Bay queen of gossip is going to find herself on the other side now. So many questions to be answered!

Xo,

Piper & Rayne

ABOUT THE AUTHOR

Piper Rayne is a USA Today Bestselling Author duo who write "heartwarming humor with a side of sizzle" about families, whether that be blood or found. They both have e-readers full of one-clickable books, they're married to husbands who drive them to drink, and they're both chauffeurs to their kids. Most of all, they love hot heroes and quirky heroines who make them laugh, and they hope you do, too!